MINDSWAP

MINDSWAP

A NOVEL BY
ROBERT SHECKLEY

DELACORTE PRESS   NEW YORK

TO PAUL KWITNEY

MINDSWAP

CHAPTER 1

MARVIN FLYNN READ THE FOLLOWING AD-
vertisement in the classified section of the *Stanhope
Gazette:*

> Gentleman from Mars, age 43, quiet, studious,
> cultured, wishes to exchange bodies with similarly
> inclined Earth gentleman. August 1–September 1.
> References Exchanged. Brokers protected.

This commonplace announcement was enough to set
Flynn's pulse racing. To swap bodies with a Martian . . .
It was an exciting idea, but also a repellent one. After all,
no one would want some sand-grubbing old Martian inside his head, moving his arms and legs, looking out of
his eyes and listening with his ears. But in return for this
unpleasantness, he, Marvin Flynn, would be able to see
Mars. And he would be able to see it as it should be seen:
through the senses of a native.

As some wish to collect paintings, others books, others

1

women, so Marvin Flynn wanted to acquire the substance of them all through travel. But this, his ruling passion, was sadly unfulfilled. He had been born and raised in Stanhope, New York. Physically, his town was some three hundred miles from New York City. But spiritually and emotionally, the two cities were about a hundred years apart.

Stanhope was a pleasing rural community situated in the foothills of the Adirondacks, garlanded with orchards and dotted with clusters of brown cows against rolling green pastureland. Invincibly bucolic, Stanhope clung to antique ways; amiably, but with a hint of pugnacity, the town kept its distance from the flinthearted megalopolis to the south. The IRT–7th Avenue subway had burrowed upstate as far as Kingston, but no farther. Gigantic freeways twisted their concrete tentacles over the countryside, but could not take over Stanhope's elm-lined Main Street. Other communities maintained a blast pit; Stanhope clung to its antiquated jet field and was content with triweekly service. (Often at night, Marvin had lain in bed and listened to that poignant sound of a vanishing rural America, the lonely wail of a jetliner.)

Stanhope was satisfied with itself, and the rest of the world seemed quite satisfied with Stanhope and willing to leave it to its romantic dream of a less hurried age. The only person whom the arrangement did not suit was Marvin Flynn.

He had gone on the usual tours and had seen the usual things. Like everyone else, he had spent many weekends in the capitals of Europe. And he had explored the sunken city of Miami by scuba, gazed at the Hanging Gardens of London, and had worshipped in the Bahai temple in Haifa. For his longer vacations, he had gone on a walking tour across Marie Byrd Land, explored the lower Ituri Rain Forest, crossed Sinkiang by camel, and had even lived for several weeks in Lhassa, the art capital of the world. In all of this, his actions were typical of his age and station.

But these trips meant nothing to him; they were the usual tourist assortment, the sort of things that any casual vacationer was likely to do. Instead of rejoicing in what he had, Flynn complained of what was denied him. He wanted to *really* travel, and that meant going extraterrestrial.

It didn't seem so much to ask; and yet, he had never even been to the Moon.

In the final analysis, it was a matter of economics. Interstellar travel was expensive; for the most part, it was confined to the rich, or to colonists and administrators. It was simply out of the question for an average sort of fellow. Unless, of course, he wished to avail himself of the advantages of Mindswap.

Flynn, with innate small-town conservatism, had avoided this logical but unsettling step. Until now.

Marvin had tried to reconcile himself to his position in life, and to the very acceptable possibilities that that position offered him. After all, he was free, gray, and thirty-one (a little over thirty-one, actually.) He was personable, a tall, broad-shouldered boy with a clipped black moustache and gentle brown eyes. He was healthy, intelligent, a good mixer, and not unacceptable to the other sex. He had received the usual education: grade school, high school, twelve years of college, and four years of postgraduate work. He was well trained for his

3

job with the Reyck-Peters Corporation. There he fluoroscoped plastic toys, subjecting them to stress analysis and examining them for microshrinkage, porosity, texture fatigue, and the like. Perhaps it wasn't the most important job in the world; but then, we can't all be kings or spaceship pilots. It was certainly a responsible position, especially when one considers the importance of toys in this world, and the vital task of alleviating the frustrations of children.

Marvin knew all this; and yet, he was unsatisfied. In vain he had gone to his neighborhood Councellor. This kindly man had tried to help Marvin through Situation Factor Analysis, but Marvin had not responded with insight. He wanted to *travel*, he refused to look honestly at the hidden implications of that desire, and he would not accept any substitutes.

And now, reading that mundane yet thrilling advertisement similar to a thousand others yet unique in its particularity (since *he* was at the moment reading it), Marvin felt a strange sensation in his throat. To swap bodies with a Martian . . . to see Mars, to visit the burrow of the Sand King, to travel through the aural splendor of The Wound, to listen to the chromatic sands of the Great Dry Sea . . .

He had dreamed before. But this time was different. That strange sensation in his throat argued a decision in the forming. Marvin wisely did not try to force it. Instead, he put on his beanie and went downtown to the Stanhope Pharmacy.

CHAPTER 2

AS HE HAD EXPECTED, HIS BEST FRIEND, Billy Hake, was at the soda fountain, sitting on a stool and drinking a mild hallucinogen known as an LSD frappe.

"How's the morn, Sorn?" Hake asked, in the slang popular at that time.

"Soft and mazy, Esterhazy," Marvin replied, giving the obligatory response.

"Du koomen ta de la klipje?" Billy asked. (Pidgin Spanish-Afrikaans dialect was the new laugh sensation that year.)

"Ja, Mijnheer," Marvin answered, a little heavily. His heart simply was not in the clever repartee.

Billy caught the nuance of dissatisfaction. He raised a quizzical eyebrow, folded his copy of James Joyce Comics, popped a Keen-Smoke into his mouth, bit down to release the fragrant green vapor, and asked, "For-why you burrow?" The question was wryly phrased but obviously well intended.

Marvin sat down beside Billy. Heavyhearted, yet unwilling to reveal his unhappiness to his lighthearted friend, he held up both hands and proceeded to speak in Plains Indian Sign Language. (Many intellectually inclined young men were still under the influence of last year's sensational Projectoscope production of *Dakota Dialogue*, starring Bjorn Rakradish as Crazy Horse and Milovar Slavovivowitz as Red Cloud, and done entirely in gesture.)

Marvin made the gestures, mocking yet serious, for heart-that-breaks, horse-that-wanders, sun-that-will-not-shine, moon-that-cannot-rise.

He was interrupted by Mr. Bigelow, proprietor of the Stanhope Pharmacy. Mr. Bigelow was a middle-aged man of seventy-four, slightly balding, with a small but evident paunch. Yet he affected boys' ways. Now he said to Marvin, "Eh, Mijnheer, querenzie tomar la klopje inmensa de la cabeza vefrouvens in forma de ein skoboldash sundae?"

It was typical of Mr. Bigelow and others of his generation to overdo the youthful slang, thus losing any comic effect except the pathetically unintentional.

"Schnell," Marvin said, putting him down with the thoughtless cruelty of youth.

"Well, I never," said Mr. Bigelow, and moved huffily away with the mincing step he had learned from the *Imitation of Life* show.

Billy perceived his friend's pain. It embarrassed him. He was thirty-four, a year and a bit older than Marvin, nearly a man. He had a good job as foreman of Assembly Line 23 in Peterson's Box Factory. He clung to adolescent ways, of course, but he knew that his age presented him with certain obligations. Thus, he crosscircuited his fear of embarrassment, and spoke to his oldest friend in clear.

6

"Marvin—what's the matter?"

Marvin shrugged his shoulder, quirked his mouth, and drummed aimlessly with his fingers. He said, "Oiga, hombre, ein Kleinnachtmusik es demasiado, nicht wahr? The Todt you ruve to touch . . ."

"Straighten it," Billy said, with a quiet dignity beyond his years.

"I'm sorry," Marvin said, in clear. "It's just—oh, Billy, I really do want to travel so badly!"

Billy nodded. He was aware of his friend's obsession. "Sure," he said. "Me too."

"But not as bad. Billy—I got the burns."

His skoboldash sundae arrived. Marvin ignored it, and poured out his heart to his lifelong friend. "Mira, Billy, it's really got me wound tighter than a plastic retriever coil. I think of Mars and Venus, and really *faraway* places like Aldeberan and Antares and—I mean, gosh, I just can't stop thinking about it all. Like the Talking Ocean of Procyon IV, and the tripartritate hominoids of Allua II, and it's like I'll simply die if I don't really and actually see those places."

"Sure," his friend said. "I'd like to see them, too."

"No, you don't *understand*," Marvin said. "It's not just to see—it's—it's like—it's worse than—I mean, I can't just *live* here in Stanhope the rest of my life even though it's fun and I got a nice job and I'm dating some really guapa girls but heck, I can't just marry some *girl* and raise kids and—and—there's gotta be something more!"

Then Marvin lapsed into adolescent incoherence. But something of his feelings had come through the wild torrent of his words, and his friend nodded sagely.

"Marvin," he said softly, "I read you five by five, honest to Sam I do. But gee, even interplanetary travel costs *fortunes*. And interstellar stuff is just plain impossible."

"It's all possible," Marvin said, "if you use Mindswap."

"Marvin! You can't mean that!" His friend was too shocked to avoid the exclamation.

"I can!" Marvin said. "And by the Christo malherido, I'm going to!"

That shocked them both. Marvin hardly ever used bad language, and his friend could see the considerable stress he was under to use such an expression, even though coded. And Marvin, having said what he had said, recognized the implacable nature of his resolve. And having expressed it, he found it less frightening to contemplate the next step, that of doing something about it.

"But you *can't*," Billy said. "Mindswap is—well, it's dirty!"

" 'Dirty he who dirty thinks, Cabrón.' "

"No, seriously. You don't want some sand-grubbing ole Martian inside your head? Moving your legs and arms, looking out of your eyes, *touching* you, and maybe even—"

Marvin cut him off before he said something really bad. "Mira," he said, "recuerda que I'll be in *his* body, on Mars, so he'll be having the same embarrassments."

"Martians haven't got no sense of embarrassment," Billy said.

"That's just not true," Marvin said. Although younger, he was in many ways more mature than his friend. He had been an apt student in Comparative Interstellar Ethics. And his intense desire to travel rendered him less provincial in his attitudes, more prepared to see the other creature's point of view, than his friend. From the age of twelve, when he had learned how to read, Marvin had studied the manners and modes of many different races

8

in the Galaxy. Always he had endeavored to view those creatures through their own eyes, and to understand their motivations in terms of their own unique psychologies. Furthermore, he had scored in the 95th percentile in Projective Empathy, thus establishing his raw potentiality for successful extraterrestrial relationships. In a word, he was as prepared for travel as it is possible for a young man to become who has lived all his life in a small town in the hinterlands of Earth.

That afternoon, alone in his attic room, Marvin opened his encyclopedia. It had been his companion and friend ever since his parents bought it for him when he was nine. Now he set the comprehension level at "simple," the skan rate at "rapid," punched his questions, and settled back as the little red and green lights flashed on.

"Hi, fellows," the tapecorder said in its fruitily enthusiastic voice. "Today—let's talk about Mindswap!"

There followed a historical section, which Marvin ignored. His attention returned when he heard the tapecorder saying:

"So let's just consider Mind as a kinda electroform or maybe even a subelectroform entity. You pro'lly remember from our previous talk that Mind is thought to have begun as a projection of our bodily processes, and to have evolved into a quasi-independent entity. You know what that means, fellas. It means it's like you got a little Man in your head—but not quite. Isn't that *quazi?*"

The tapecorder laughed modestly at its little joke, then went on.

"So what have we got out of this mishmash? Well, kids, we got ourselves a sort of symbiotic situation, mind and bodywise, even though Mr. Mind is inclined to a sort of

9

parasitism. But still, each can exist—theoretically—without the other. Or anyhow, that's what the Big Thinkers say."

Marvin skimmed.

"Now as for projecting the mind—well, guys, just think of throwing a ball . . ."

"Mental into physical, and vice versa. Ultimately, they are forms of each other, just like matter and energy. Of course, we have yet to discover . . ."

"But of course, we have only a pragmatic knowledge of it. We might consider, just for a very brief moment, Van Voorhes' concept of Agglutinative Reform, and the Lagos University Theory of Relative Absolutes. Of course, these theories raise more questions than they answer. . . ."

". . . and the whole works is made possible only by the somewhat surprising lack of an immuniform reaction."

"The actual practice of Mindswap utilizes mechanical-hypnotic techniques such as induced relaxation, pinpoint fixation, and the use of a mind-positive substance, such as Williamite, as a narrow-beam focuser and intensifier. Feedback programming . . ."

"Once learned, of course, you can Swap without mechanical aids, usually employing sight as focus . . ."

Marvin turned off the encyclopedia and thought about space, and the many planets, and the exotic inhabitants of those planets. He thought about Mindswap. He thought: Tomorrow I could be on Mars. Tomorrow I could be a Martian. . . .

He jumped to his feet. "By jingo!" he cried, striking palm of his left hand with his right fist, "I'll do it!"

The strange alchemy of decision had transformed him. Without hesitation he packed a light suitcase, left a note for his parents, and caught the jet to New York.

CHAPTER 3

IN NEW YORK, MARVIN WENT DIRECTLY TO the body-brokerage house of Otis, Blanders and Klent. He was sent to the office of Mr. Blanders, a tall, athletic man in the prime of life at sixty-three, and a full partner in the firm. He explained to this man his purpose in coming.

"Of course," Mr. Blanders said. "You have reference to our advertisement of Friday last. The Martian gentleman's name is Ze Kraggash, and he is very highly recommended by the rectors of East Skern University."

"What does he look like?" Marvin asked.

"See for yourself," Blanders said. He showed Marvin a photograph of a being with a barrel chest, thin legs, slightly thicker arms, and a small head with an extremely long nose. The picture showed Kraggash standing knee-deep in mud, waving to someone. Printed on the bottom of the photograph were the words: "Souvenir of Mud Heaven—Mars' Year-'Round Vacationland, highest moisture content on the planet!"

"Nice-looking chap," Mr. Blanders commented. Marvin nodded, even though Kraggash looked just like any other Martian to him.

"His home," Blanders continued, "is in Wagomstamk, which is on the edge of the Disappearing Desert in New South Mars. It is an extremely popular tourist area, as you probably know. Like you, Mr. Kraggash is desirous of traveling and wishes to find a suitable host body. He has left the selection entirely up to us, stipulating only mental and physical health."

"Well," Marvin said, "I don't mean to boast, but I've always been considered healthy."

"I can see that at a glance," Mr. Blanders said. "It is only a feeling, of course, or perhaps an intuition, but I have come to trust my feelings in thirty years of dealing with the public. Purely on the basis of my feelings, I have rejected the last three applicants for this particular Swap."

Mr. Blanders seemed so proud of this that Marvin felt impelled to say, "Have you really?"

"Most certainly. You can have no conception of how frequently I must detect and eliminate misfits in this line of work. Neurotics who seek ugly and illicit thrills; criminals who wish to escape the purview of local law; the mentally unstable, trying to escape their internal psychic pressures. And many more. I cull them all."

"I hope that I don't fit any of those categories," Marvin said, with an embarrassed little laugh.

"I can tell at once that you do not," Mr. Blanders said. "I would judge you as an extremely normal young man, almost *excessively* normal, if that were possible. You have been bitten by the travel bug, which is very suitable

12

for your time of life, and is a passion akin to falling in love, or fighting an idealistic war, or becoming disillusioned with the world, and other postures of the young. It is very fortunate that you had either the native wit or the good luck to come to us, the oldest and most reliable brokerage house in the Swap business, rather than to some of our less scrupulous competitors, or, worst of all, to the Open Market."

Marvin knew very little about the Open Market; but he remained silent, not wishing to betray his ignorance by asking.

"Now then," Mr. Blanders said, "we have certain formalities which we must go through before we can gratify your request."

"Formalities?" Marvin asked.

"Most certainly. First, you must have a complete examination, which will produce an operational judgment of your physical, mental, and moral standing. This is quite necessary, since bodies are swapped on an equal basis. You would be quite unhappy if you found yourself stuck in the corpus of a Martian suffering from sandpest or tunnel syndrome. Just as he would be unhappy if he found that you had rickets or paranoia. By the terms of our charter, we must attempt as complete a knowledge of the health and stability of the Swappers as possible, and apprise them of any discrepancies between real and advertised condition."

"I see," Marvin said. "And what happens after that?"

"Next, you and the Martian Gentleman will both sign a Reciprocal Damage Clause. This states that any damage to your host body, whether by omission or commission, and including Acts of God, will, one, be recompensed at

13

the rate established by interstellar convention, and, two, that such damage will be visited reciprocally upon your own body in accordance with the *lex talionis*."

"Huh?" Marvin said.

"Eye for eye, tooth for tooth," Mr. Blanders explained. "It's really quite simple enough. Suppose you, in the Martian corpus, break a leg on the last day of Occupancy. You suffer the pain, to be sure, but not the subsequent inconvenience, which you avoid by returning to your own undamaged body. But this is not equitable. Why should you escape the consequences of your own accident? Why should someone else suffer those consequences for you? So, in the interests of justice, interstellar law requires that, upon reoccupying your own body, your own leg be broken in as scientific and painless a manner as possible."

"Even if the first broken leg was an accident?"

"*Especially* if it were an accident. We have found that the Reciprocal Damage Clause has cut down the number of such accidents quite considerably."

"This begins to sound sorta dangerous," Marvin said.

"Any course of action contains an element of danger," Mr. Blanders said. "But the risks involved in Swapping are statistically unimportant, assuming that you stay out of the Twisted World."

"I don't know very much about the Twisted World," Marvin said.

"Nobody does," Blanders said. "That's why you're supposed to stay out of it. That's reasonable enough, isn't it?"

"I suppose so," Marvin said. "What else is there?"

"Nothing to speak of. Just paperwork, waivers of spe-

14

cial rights and immunities, that sort of thing. And, of course, I must give you the standard warning about metaphoric deformation."

"All right," Marvin said. "I'd like to hear it."

"I just gave it," Blanders said. "But I'll give it again. Watch out for metaphoric deformation."

"I'd be glad to," Marvin said, "but I don't know what it is."

"It's really quite simple," Blanders said. "You might consider it a form of situational insanity. You see, our ability to assimilate the unusual is limited, and these limits are quickly reached and surpassed when we travel to alien planets. We experience too much novelty; it becomes unbearable, and the mind seeks relief through the buffering process of analogizing.

"Analogy assures us that *this* is like *that;* it forms a bridge between the accepted known and the unacceptable unknown. It attaches the one to the other, imbuing the intolerable unknown with a desirable familiarity.

"However, under the continued and unremitting impact of the unknown, even the analogizing faculty can become distorted. Unable to handle the flood of data by the normal process of conceptual analogizing, the subject becomes victim to *perceptual* analogizing. This state is what we call 'metaphoric deformation.' The process is also known as 'Panzaism.' Does that make it clear?"

"No," Marvin said. "Why is it called 'Panzaism'?"

"The concept is self-explanatory," Blanders said. "Don Quijote thinks the windmill is a giant, whereas Panza thinks the giant is a windmill. Quijotism may be defined as the perception of everyday things as rare entities. The

15

reverse of that is Panzaism, which is the perception of rare entities as everyday things."

"Do you mean," Marvin asked, "that I might think I was looking at a cow, when actually it was an Altairian?"

"Precisely," Blanders said. "It's simple enough, once you apply yourself. Just sign here and here and we will get on with the examinations."

There were many tests, and endless questions. Flynn was poked and probed, lights were flashed in his face, sudden noises were broadcast at him, and strange smells assailed his nostrils.

He passed everything with flying colors. Some hours later he was taken to the Transfer Room, and was seated in a chair that looked alarmingly like an old electric chair. The technicians made obligatory jokes: "When you wake up, you'll feel like a new man." Lights flashed at him, he was getting sleepy, sleepier, sleepiest.

He was thrilled by the imminence of travel, but appalled by his ignorance of the world beyond Stanhope. What was the Open Market, anyhow? Where was the Twisted World located, and why was he supposed to avoid it? And finally, how dangerous was metaphoric deformation, how often did it occur, and what was the recovery rate?

Soon he would find the answers to these questions, as well as the answers to many others that he hadn't asked. The lights were hurting his eyes, and he closed them for a moment. When he opened them again, everything had changed.

CHAPTER 4

DESPITE A BIPEDAL FRAME, THE MARTIAN is one of the strangest creatures in the galaxy. Indeed, from a sensory viewpoint, the Kvees of Aldeberan, despite their double brains and special-function limbs, are closer to us. Accordingly, it is a disturbing thing to Swap directly and without initiation into the corpus of a Martian. And yet, no amelioration is possible.

Marvin Flynn found himself in a pleasantly furnished room. There was a single window; through it, he gazed with Martian eyes upon a Martian landscape.

He closed his eyes, since he could register nothing except a dismaying confusion. Despite innoculations, he was beset by the nausea-producing waves of culture-shock, and he had to stand very still until it subsided. Then, cautiously, he opened his eyes and looked again.

He perceived low, flat sand dunes, which were made up of a hundred or more distinct hues of gray. A silvery-blue wind was running across the horizon, and an ochre counterwind seemed to be attacking it. The sky was red, and many indescribable hues were visible in the infrared scale. In everything, Flynn saw spidery spectrum lines. Earth and sky presented him with a dozen separate palettes, some complementary, more of them clashing. There was no harmony in nature's colors on Mars; these were the colors of chaos.

Marvin found a pair of glasses in his hand, and slipped them on. Immediately, the roar and clash of colors was reduced to manageable proportions. The numbness of shock receded, and he began to perceive other things.

First, a heavy booming in his ear, and a quick rattle beneath it, like the tattoo of a snare drum. He looked around for the source of this noise, and saw nothing except earth and sky. He listened more carefully, and found that the sounds were coming from his own chest. They were his lungs and heart, sounds that all Martians lived with.

Now Marvin was able to take stock of himself. He looked at his legs, which were long and spindly. There was no knee joint; instead, the leg was pivoted at the ankle, shin, midthigh, and upper thigh. He walked, and admired the fluid motion of his movements. His arms were slightly thicker than his legs, and his double-jointed hands had three fingers and two opposable thumbs. He could bend and twist these in a surprising number of ways.

He was dressed in black shorts and a white jumper. His chest-prop was folded neatly and covered with an embroidered leather case. He was amazed at how natural it all seemed.

And yet, it was not surprising. The ability of intelligent

18

creatures to accommodate to new environments was what made Mindswap possible. And the Martian frame, despite certain striking morphological and sensory differences, was easy to get used to, unlike some of nature's more perverse creations.

Flynn was musing on this when he heard a door open behind him. He turned and saw a Martian standing in front of him, dressed in a government uniform of green and gray stripes. The Martian had reversed his feet in greeting, and Marvin quickly responded in kind.

(One of the glories of Mindswap is "automatic education." Or, in the amusing jargon of the trade: "When you take over a house, you get the use of the furnishings." The furnishings, of course, are the use of primary available knowledge in the host-brain, knowledge such as language, customs, mores and morals, general information about the area in which one lives, and so forth. This is primary-environment information, general, impersonal, useful as a guide, but not necessarily reliable. Personal memories, likes, dislikes are, with certain exceptions, unavailable to the occupier, or available only at the cost of considerable mental effort. Again, in this area there is what appears to be a type of immunilogical reaction, which allows only a superficial degree of contact between disparate entities. "General knowledge" is usually exempt; but "personal knowledge," involving beliefs, prejudices, hopes and fears is sacrosanct.)

"Soft wind," the Martian said, in the classic old-Martian greeting form.

"And cloudless sky," Flynn replied. (To his annoyance, he found that his host-body had a slight lisp.)

19

"I am Meenglo Orichichich, of the Tourist Bureau. Welcome to Mars, Mr. Flynn."

"Thanks," Flynn said. "Awfully good to be here. It's my first Swap, you know."

"Yes, I know," Orichichich said. He spat on the floor—a sure sign of nervousness—and uncurled his thumbs. From the corridor there came a sound of heavy voices. Orichichich said, "Now then, concerning your stay on Mars—"

"I want to see the Burrow of the Sand King," Flynn said. "And, of course, the Talking Ocean."

"Both excellent choices," the official said. "But first there are one or two minor formalities."

"Formalities?"

"Nothing too difficult," Orichichich said, his nose twisting to the left in the Martian smile. "Would you look over these papers and identify them, please?"

Flynn took the proferred papers and scanned them. They were replicas of the forms he had signed on Earth. He read them through, and found that all the information had been sent correctly.

"These are the papers I signed on Earth," he said.

The noise from the corridor grew louder. Marvin could make out words: "Scalded egg-laying son of a frostbitten tree stump! Gravel-loving degenerate!"

Those were very strong insults indeed.

Marvin raised his nose quizzically. The official hastily said, "A misunderstanding, a mixup. One of those unfortunate occurrences which occur even to the best-run of government tourist services. But I am quite sure that we can straighten it out in five gulps of a rapi, if not sooner. Permit me to ask you if—"

There was the sound of a scuffle in the corridor. Then a Martian burst into the room, with a Martian subofficial clinging to his arm and trying to stop him.

The Martian who had burst in was extremely old, as could be told by the faint phosphorescence of his skin. His arms quivered as he pointed both of them at Marvin Flynn.

"There!" he shouted. "There it is, and by treestumps I want it now!"

Marvin said, "Sir, I am not in the habit of being addressed as 'it'."

"I am not addressing you," the old Martian said. "I do not know nor care who or what you are. I am addressing the body which you are occupying, and which is not yours."

"What are you talking about?" Flynn asked.

"This gentleman," the official said, "claims that you are occupying a body which belongs to him." He spat twice on the floor. "It is a mixup, of course, and we can straighten it out at once. . . ."

"Mixup!" howled the old Martian. "It's an out-and-out fraud!"

"Sir," Marvin said, with cold dignity, "you are under a grave misapprehension; either that, or you are engaging in this slander for reasons I cannot hope to fathom. This body, sir, was legally and fairly rented by me."

"Scaly-skinned toad!" the old man shouted. "Let me at him!" He struggled with circumspection against the restraining grip of the guard.

Suddenly, an imposing figure dressed entirely in white appeared in the doorway. All within the room fell silent as their gaze fell upon the feared and respected representative of the South Martian Desert Police.

"Gentlemen," the policeman said, "there is no need for recriminations. We shall proceed now to the police station, all of us. There, with the help of the Fulszime telepath, we shall penetrate to the truth, and to the motivation behind it." The policeman paused impressively, stared full into each man's face, swallowed saliva to show supreme calm, and said: "This, I promise you."

Without further ado the policeman, the official, the old man, and Marvin Flynn proceeded to the police station. They walked silently, and they shared a common mood of apprehension. It is a truism throughout the civilized galaxy that when you go to the police, your troubles really begin.

CHAPTER 5

AT THE POLICE STATION, MARVIN FLYNN and the others were taken directly to the dim, moist chamber where the Fulszime telepath lived. This tripedal entity, like all of his fellows from the Fulszime Planet, possessed a telepathic sixth sense, perhaps in compensation for the dimness of his other five.

"All right," the Fulszime telepath said, when all were assembled before him. "Step forward, fellow, and tell me your story." He pointed a finger sternly at the policeman.

"Sir!" the policeman said, straightening with embarrassment, "I happen to be the policeman."

"That is interesting," the telepath said. "But I fail to see what it has to do with the question of your innocence or guilt."

"But I am not even accused of a crime," the policeman said.

The telepath mused for a moment, then said, "I think I

understand. . . . It is these two who are accused. Is that it?"

"It is," the policeman said.

"My apologies. Your aura of guilt led me to an over-hasty identification."

"Guilt?" the policeman said. "Me?" He spoke calmly, but his skin was showing the typical orange striations of anxiety.

"Yes, you," the telepath said. "You need not be surprised; grand larceny is the sort of thing about which most intelligent creatures feel guilty."

"Now just a minute!" the policeman shouted. "I haven't committed any grand larceny!"

The telepath closed his eyes and introspected. At last he said, "That is correct. I meant to say that you *will* perform grand larceny."

"Clairvoyance is not admissable as evidence in a court of law," the policeman stated. "And furthermore, readings of the future are a direct violation of the law of free will."

"This is true," the telepath said. "My apologies."

"It's quite all right," the policeman said. "When will I perform this alleged grand larceny?"

"About six months hence," the telepath said.

"And will I be arrested?"

"No. You will flee the planet, going to a place where there is no extradition law."

"Hmm, interesting," the policeman said. "Could you tell me if . . . But we can discuss this later. Now, you must hear the stories of these men, and judge their innocence or guilt."

The telepath looked at Marvin, shook a flipper at him,

24

and said, "You may proceed." Marvin told his story, beginning with his first reading of the advertisement and leaving out nothing.

"Thank you," the telepath said, when he was through. "And now, sir, your story." He turned to the old Martian, who cleared his throat, scratched his thorax, spit once or twice, and then proceeded.

AIGELER THRUS'S STORY

I don't even know where to begin this thing, so I guess I'd better start with my name, which is Aigeler Thrus, and my race, which is Nemucthian Adventist, and my occupation, which is that I own and operate a clothing store on the planet Achelses V. Well, it's a small business and not a very good business and my store is located in Lambersa on the South Polar Cap, and I sell clothing all day to immigrant Venusian laborers, who are big, green, hairy fellows, very ignorant and very excitable and apt to fight, though I have no prejudices against them.

You get to be philosophical in my business, and maybe I'm not rich, but at least I got my health (thank God), and my wife Allura is healthy too except for a mild case of tentacular fibrosis. And I got two grown sons, one of whom is a doctor in Sidneport, and the other is a trainer of Klannts. And I also got one daughter, who is married, so of course that means I got a son-in-law.

This son-in-law of mine I have always distrusted, since he is a fancy dresser and owns twenty pairs of chest-props, although his wife my daughter hasn't even got a matched set of scratchers. But it can't be helped, she dug her burrow, now she has to crawl in it. But still, when a man is so interested in clothes and fancy-smelling joint lubricants and similar luxuries on the salary of a moisture salesman (he calls himself a "hydrosensory engineer") it makes you wonder a little.

And he's always trying to scratch up extra income on the side with various foolish ventures, which I have to equip him for out of my hard-earned savings, which I get by selling to these big green fellows. Like last year he got hold of this novelty item, a backyard cloudmaker, and I told him, who would want it? But my wife insisted that I help him out, and sure enough he went broke. And then this year, he had another scheme, and this time it was iridescent synthetic wool seconds from Vega II, a consignment of which he somehow found in Heligoport and which he wanted me to buy.

I said to him, "Look, what do my customers these Venusian loudmouths know about fancy dressing? They're lucky if they can afford a pair of twill shorts and maybe a robe for holidays." But my son-in-law has got an answer for everything and he says to me, "Look, Papa, have I or have I not made a study of Venusian folkways and mores? The way I look at it, here are these people straight out of the backwoods, and they've got this love of ritual and dance and *bright colors*. So it's a natural, true or not?"

Well, to make a short story even shorter, I get talked into this venture against my better judgment. Naturally, I had to see those iridescent seconds myself, because I wouldn't trust my son-in-law to judge a piece of lint. And that meant traveling halfway across the galaxy to Heligoport in Mars. So I started making the arrangements.

No one wanted to Swap with me. I can't say I blame them, because nobody comes on purpose to a planet like

Achelses V, unless it's immigrant Venusians who don't know any better. But I find this ad from this Martian, Ze Kraggash, who wants to rent his body out on account of he's taking his mind into Cold Storage for a protracted rest. It's damned expensive, but what can I do? I get a little money back by renting my own body to a friend who had been a quarentz hunter before he was bedridden by muscular dyscomyotosis. And I go down to the Swap Bureau and get projected to Mars.

Well, imagine my sensations when it turns out there is no body waiting for me! Everybody's running around trying to find out what happened to my host-body, and they even try to send me back to Achelses V; but they can't because my friend has already left on a quarentz hunting expedition with my body.

Finally they get me a body from the Theresiendstadt Rent-a-Body people. Twelve hours is the maximum they can allow me since they're all booked up for short-term rentals through the summer. And it's a pretty decrepit old body, as you can see for yourself, and damned expensive anyhow.

So I go out and try to find out what had gone wrong, and what do I find but this tourist from Earth walking around bold as brass in the body which I have paid for, and which, according to my contract, I should be occupying at this very moment.

It is not only unfair, it is also extremely aggravating to my health. And that is the entire story.

The telepath retired to his chambers in order to ponder his decision. He returned in less than an hour and spoke as follows:

"Both of you did, in all good faith, rent, swap, or otherwise acquire, the same body, viz., the corpus of Ze Kraggash. This body was offered by its owner, the aforesaid Ze Kraggash, to each of you, and thus sale was consummated in direct violation of all laws concerned. Ze Kraggash's action must be considered criminal, both in execution and intent. This being the case, I have caused to be sent to Earth a message, requesting the immediate arrest of the aforesaid Ze Kraggash, and his detention in a place of custody until such time as his extradition can be effected.

"Both of you made your purchase in good faith; however, the prior, or earlier, sale, as shown in the contractual forms, was made by Mr. Aigeler Thrus, who takes precedence over Mr. Marvin Flynn by a matter of thirty-eight hours. Therefore Mr. Thrus, as the First Buyer, is awarded custody of the Corpus; and Mr. Flynn is ordered to cease and desist his unlawful occupancy, and to take cognizance of the Dispossess Notice, which I hereby give him, and which must be obeyed within six standard Greenwich hours."

The telepath handed Marvin a Dispossess Notice. Flynn accepted it sadly, yet with resignation. "I suppose," he said, "that I had better go back to my own body on Earth."

"That," the telepath said, "would be your wisest choice. Unfortunately, it is not possible at the moment."

"Not possible? Why not?"

"Because," the telepath said, "according to the Earth authorities, whose telepathic reply I have just received, your body, animated by the mind of Ze Kraggash, is nowhere to be found. A preliminary investigation leads us to fear that Ze Kraggash has fled the planet, taking with him your body and Mr. Aigeler's money."

It took a while for it to sink in, but finally, Marvin Flynn realized the implications of what had been said. He was stranded on Mars in an alien body, which he had to relinquish. In six hours, he would be a mind with no body at all and with a poor chance of finding one.

Minds cannot exist without bodies. Marvin Flynn slowly and unwillingly faced the imminence of his own death.

CHAPTER 6

MARVIN DID NOT GIVE WAY TO DESPAIR. HE gave way instead to anger, which was a much healthier emotion, though equally unproductive. Instead of making a fool of himself by weeping in the court, he made a fool of himself by storming through the corridors of the Federal Building, demanding either fair play or a damned good substitute.

There was no restraining this impetuous young man. Quite in vain did several lawyers point out to him that, if justice really existed, there would be no need for law and lawmakers, and thus one of mankind's noblest conceptions would be obliterated, and an entire occupational group would be thrown out of work. For it is the essence of the law, they told him, that abuses and outrages should exist, since these discrepancies served as proof and validation of the necessity of law, and of justice itself.

This lucid argument brought no peace to the frenzied Marvin, who gave every appearance of a man insusceptible to reason. The breath rasped and rattled in his throat as he roared his contempt for the Justice machinery of Mars. His behavior was considered disgraceful and was tolerated only because he was young and therefore not fully acculturated.

But rage brought him no results and did not even produce in him the healthy sensations of catharsis. Several judicial clerks pointed this out to him and were mercilessly snubbed for their efforts.

Marvin remained unaware of the bad impression he was creating in the minds of others, and after a while his anger spent itself, leaving as its residue a sullen resentment.

It was in this mood that he came to a door marked "Bureau of Detection and Apprehension, Interstellar Division."

"Aha!" Marvin muttered, and entered the office.

He found himself in a small room that looked like something out of the pages of an old historical novel. Against the wall were dignified banks of old but reliable electronic calculators. Near the door was an early-model thought-to-print translator. The armchairs had the abrupt shape and pastel plastic upholstery that we associate with a more leisurely era. The room lacked only a bulky solid-state Moraeny to make it a perfect replica of a scene from the pages of Sheckley or one of the other early poets of the Age of Transmission.

There was a middle-aged Martian seated in a chair throwing darts at a target shaped like a woman's bottom.

He turned hastily when Marvin came in and said, "It's about time. I was expecting you."

32

"Were you really?" Marvin asked.

"Well, not really," the Martian said. "But I have found that it makes an effective opening and tends to create an atmosphere of trust."

"Then why do you ruin it by telling me?"

The Martian shrugged his shoulder and said, "Look, no one's perfect. I'm just an ordinary working detective. Urf Urdorf's the name. Sit down. I think we have a lead on your missing fur coat."

"What fur coat?" Marvin asked.

"Aren't you Madame Ripper de Lowe, the transvestite who was robbed last night in the Red Sands Hotel?"

"Certainly not. I'm Marvin Flynn, and I lost my body."

"Of course, of course," Detective Urdorf said, nodding vigorously. "Let's take it point by point. Do you remember by any chance where you were when you first noticed that your body was missing? Could any of your friends have taken it as a joke? Or could you have merely misplaced it, or perhaps sent it on a vacation?"

"I didn't really *lose* it," Marvin said. "Actually, it was stolen."

"You should have said so in the first place," Urdorf said. "That tends to put the matter in a different light. I am only a detective; I have never claimed to be a mind-reader."

"I'm sorry," Marvin said.

"I'm sorry, too," Detective Urdorf said. "About your body, I mean. It must have been quite a nasty shock."

"Yes, it was."

"I can well understand how you feel."

"Thank you," Marvin said.

They sat in companionable silence for several minutes. Then Marvin said, "Well?"

"I beg your pardon?" the detective replied.

"I said, 'Well?'"

"Oh. I'm sorry, I'm afraid I didn't hear you the first time."

"That's quite all right."

"Thank you."

"You're extremely welcome."

There was another silence. Then Marvin said, "Well?" once again, and Urdorf said, "I beg your pardon?"

Marvin said, "I want it back."

"What?"

"My body."

"Your what? Oh yes, your body. Hmm, I dare say you do," the detective said with an appreciative smile. "But of course, it isn't as easy as that, is it?"

"I wouldn't know," Marvin said.

"No, I don't suppose you would," Urdorf said. "But I can assure you that it isn't as easy as that."

"I see," Marvin said.

"I rather hoped you would," Urdorf said, and lapsed into silence.

This silence lasted for approximately twenty-five seconds, give or take a second or two. At the end of that time Marvin's patience collapsed and he shouted, "Goddamn it are you going to do something about getting me back my body or are you going to just sit there on your goddamned fat ass and talk without saying anything?"

"Of course I am going to get you your body," the detective said. "Or, in any case, I am going to try. And there is no reason for abuse. I am not, after all, some machine filled with tabulated answers. I am an intelligent being just like yourself, I have my own hopes and fears; and, more germane, I have my own way of conducting an interview. This way may seem ineffectual to you, but I have found it extremely useful."

"Have you really?" asked Marvin, chastened.

"Why, yes, as a matter of fact I have," the detective replied, his mild voice showing no trace of rancor."

Another silence seemed about to begin, so Marvin asked, "What sort of chance do you think I have—we have—for recovering my body?"

"A most excellent chance," Detective Urdorf replied. "It is my firm belief that we will find your body soon. In fact, I think I could go so far as to say that I am certain of success. I base this not on a study of your particular case, about which I know very little at present, but on a simple examination of the statistics involved."

"Do the statistics favor us?" Marvin asked.

"They most assuredly do. Consider: I am a trained detective, conversant with all the new methods and possessing a top efficiency rating of AA-A. Yet in spite of this, during my five years with the force, I have never solved a case."

"Not a single one?"

"Not a single one," Urdorf said firmly. "Interesting, isn't it?"

"Yes, I suppose it is," Marvin said. "But doesn't that mean—"

"It means," the detective said, "that one of the strangest runs of bad luck that I have ever heard of is statistically due to break."

Marvin was nonplussed, which is an unusual sensation

in a Martian body. He said, "But suppose your luck doesn't break?"

"You must not be superstitious," the detective replied. "The probabilities are there; even the most casual examination of the situation should convince you of that. I have been unable to solve 158 cases in a row. You are my 159th. How would you bet if you were a betting man?"

"I'd stay with the run," Marvin said.

"So would I," the detective admitted, with a self-deprecating smile. "But we would both be wrong, and would be betting on the basis of our emotions rather than on the calculations of our intellect." Urdorf looked at the ceiling dreamily. "One hundred and fifty-eight failures! It's a fantastic record, an unbelievable record, especially if you grant my incorruptability, good faith, and skill. One hundred fifty-eight! A run like that simply has to break! I could probably sit here in my office and do nothing, and the criminal would find his way to me. That's how strong the probabilities are in my favor."

"Yes, sir," Marvin said politely. "But I hope you won't test that particular approach."

"No, no, of course not," Urdorf said. "It would be interesting, but some people might not understand. No, I shall pursue your case actively, especially since it is a sex crime, which is the sort of thing I am interested in."

"I beg your pardon?" Marvin said.

"There is really no need to apologize," the detective assured him. "One should not be embarrassed or guilty by reason of being the victim of a sex crime, even though the deepest folk wisdom of many cultures attaches a stigma to being such a victim, on the presumption of conscious or unconscious complicity."

36

"No, no, I wasn't apologizing," Marvin said. "I was merely—"

"I quite understand," the detective said. "But you mustn't be ashamed to tell me all the bizarre and loathsome details. You must think of me as an impersonal official function instead of as an intelligent being with sexual feeling and fears and urges and quirks and desires of his own."

"What I was trying to tell you," Marvin said, "is that there is no sex crime involved here."

"They all say that," the detective mused. "It is strange how the human mind is forever unwilling to accept the unacceptable."

"Look," Marvin said, "if you would take the time to read over the facts of the case, you would see that it was a case of an outright swindle. Money and self-perpetuation were the motives."

"I am aware of that," the detective said. "And, were I unaware of the processes of sublimation, we could leave it at that."

"What possible motive could the criminal have had?" Marvin asked.

"His motive is obvious," Urdorf said. "It is a classic syndrome. You see, this fellow was acting under a specific compulsion, for which we have a specific technical term. He was driven to his deed in an advanced state of obsessive projective narcissism."

"I don't understand," Marvin said.

"It is not the sort of thing which the layman is apt to encounter," the detective told him.

"What does it mean?"

"Well, I can't go into the entire etiology, but essentially, the dynamics of the syndrome involve a displaced self-love. That is to say, the sufferer falls in love with another, but not *as* other. Rather, he falls in love with the Other as Himself. He projects himself into the persona of the Other, identifying himself with that Other in all ways, and repudiating his actual self. And, should he be able to possess that Other, through Mindswap or allied means, then that Other becomes himself, for whom he then feels a perfectly normal self-love."

"Do you mean," Marvin asked, "that this thief loved me?"

"Not at all! Or rather, he didn't love you as *you*—as a separate person. He loved *himself* as you, and thus his neurosis forced him to *become* you in order that he could love himself."

"And once he was me," Marvin asked, "he was then able to love himself?"

"Precisely! That particular phenomenon is known as the incrementation of the ego. Possession of the Other equals possession of the primordial Self; possession becomes self-possession, obsessive projection is transformed into normative introjection. Upon achievement of the neurotic goal there is an apparent remission of symptoms, and the sufferer achieves a state of pseudonormalcy in which his problem can be detected only inferentially. It is a very great tragedy, of course."

"For the victim?"

"Well, yes, that certainly," Urdorf said. "But I was thinking of the patient. You see, in his case two perfectly normal drives have been combined, or crossed, and thus perverted. Self-love is normal and necessary, and so is the desire for possession and transformation. But taken together, they are destructive of the true self, which is supplanted by what we term the 'mirror-ego.' The neurotic conquest, you see, shuts the door to objective reality. Ironically enough, the apparent integration of the self precludes any hope of real mental health."

"All right," Marvin said, with resignation. "Will this help us find the man who stole my body?"

"It will enable us to understand him," the detective said. "Knowledge is power; we know at the very start that the man we seek is apt to act normal. This extends our field of action and enables *us* to act *as if he were normal*, and thus to see the full complement of modern investigative techniques. Being able to start from a premise like that, or indeed from any premise, is a very real advantage, I can assure you."

"How soon can you begin?" Marvin asked.

"I have already begun," the detective replied. I shall send for the court records, of course, and all other documents pertaining to this matter, and I shall contact all relevant planetary authorities for additional information. I will spare no effort, and I will travel to the ends of the universe if necessary or desirable. I shall solve this case!"

"I'm very glad you feel that way," Marvin said.

"One hundred and fifty-eight cases without a break," Urdorf mused. "Have you ever heard of such a run of bad luck? But it will end here. I mean to say, it can't go on indefinitely, can it?"

"I don't suppose so."

"I wish my superiors would take that view," the detective said gloomily. "I wish they'd stop calling me 'stumblebum.' Words like that and sneers and lifted eyebrows all tend to shake one's confidence. Luckily for me, I have

39

an implacable will and utter self-confidence. Or at least I did have through my first ninety or so failures."

The detective brooded darkly for several moments, then said to Marvin: "I will expect your complete and utter cooperation."

"You shall have it," Marvin said. "The only trouble is, I am to be dispossessed of this body in less than six hours."

"Damned awkward," Urdorf said absentmindedly. He was obviously thinking about his case, and only with difficulty did he turn his attention back to Marvin. "Dispossessed, eh? I suppose you've made other arrangements. No? Well then, I suppose you *will* make other arrangements."

"I don't know what arrangements to make," Marvin said gloomily.

"Well, you can't expect me to sort out your whole life for you," the detective snapped. "I've been trained to do one job, and the fact that I've failed consistently at it doesn't alter the fact that it *is* the job which I have been trained for. So you must cope with this matter of finding a body for yourself. The stakes are very high, you know."

"I know," Marvin said. "Finding a body is life or death for me."

"Well, yes, that too," the detective said. "But I was thinking of the case and of the detrimental effect your death would have upon it."

"That's a hell of a thing to say," Marvin said.

"I wasn't thinking of my own stake in the matter," the detective said. "Obviously, I *do* have a stake. But more important than that is the concept of Justice, and the belief in the possibility of goodness upon which all theories of evil must depend, and also the statistical theory of probabilities. All of these vital concepts might be damaged by my 159th failure to solve a crime. And I think you'll admit that these are somewhat larger issues than our petty lives."

"No, I won't admit it," Marvin said.

"Well, no need to argue the matter," the detective said, in a determinedly cheerful voice. "Find yourself another body somewhere; and above all, stay alive! I want you to promise me that you'll really try your level best to stay alive."

"I promise," Marvin said.

"And I shall proceed with your case, and I will contact you as soon as I have anything to report."

"But how will you find me?" Marvin asked. "I don't know what body I'll be in, or even what planet."

"You forget that I am a detcetive," Urdorf said, smiling faintly. "I may have my troubles in finding criminals, but I have never experienced the slightest difficulty in finding victims. I have a theory about that, which I will be pleased to discuss with you whenever we both have the time. But for now, just remember: wherever you are or whatever you turn into, I shall certainly locate you. So keep your chin up, don't lose the old moxie, and above all, stay alive!"

Marvin agreed to stay alive, since he had planned on it anyhow. And he went out into the street with his precious time flowing away, and still without a body.

CHAPTER 7

HEADLINE IN THE MARTIAN SUN-NEWS
(tri-planet edition):

SWAP SCANDAL!

Police officials on Mars and Terra revealed today the existence of a Mindswap scandal. Wanted for questioning is Ze Kraggash, species unknown, who allegedly sold, swapped, or otherwise disposed of his Body to 12 Beings simultaneously. Warrants have been issued for Kraggash's arrest, and the police of the tri-planet area confidently expect to make an announcement soon. The case is reminiscent of the infamous "Eddie Two-Head" scandal of the early '90's, in which . . .

Marvin Flynn let the newspaper fall into the gutter. He watched as the flowing sand bore it away; the bitter ephemerality of the newsprint seemed a paradigm of his

43

own highly conditional existence. He stared at his hands; his head drooped.

" 'Ere now, 'ere now, what seems to be the trouble, eh, lad?"

Flynn looked up into the kindly blue-green face of an Erlan.

"I've got troubles," Flynn said.

"Well then, let's hear 'em," the Erlan said, folding himself down on the curb beside Flynn. Like all of his race, the Erlan combined a quick sympathy with brusque manners. Erlans were known as a rough, witty people, much given to cheerful banter and homely sayings. Great travelers and traders, the Erlans of Erlan II were religiously required to travel *in corpore*.

Marvin told his story, right up to the disconsolate moment of the forward-surging *now*, the cruel and remorseless now, the hungry now, eating into his little stock of minutes and seconds, pressing forward to the time when his six hours would have elapsed, and bodyless, he would be cast into that unknown galaxy that men call "death."

"Garn!" the Erlan said. "Not half sorry for yourself, are you?"

"You're damned right I'm sorry for myself," Flynn said, with a flash of anger. "I'd be sorry for anyone who was going to die in six hours. Why shouldn't I be sorry for myself?"

"Suit yourself, cook," the Erlan said. "Some might call it bad form and all the bumf, but me, I hold with the teachings of the Guajuoie, who said; 'Is it death which snuffles near you? Strike it on the snout!' "

Marvin respected all religions, and certainly had no

44

prejudices against the widespread Antidescantine Rite. But he couldn't see how the Guajuoie's words could help him, and he said so.

"Buck up!" the Erlan said. "Got yer brains and yer six hours, ain't yer?"

"Five hours."

"Well then! Git up on your hind legs and show a little grit, eh, cobber? Won't do yourself much good maundering around here like a bloody buggering old lag, will you now?"

"I don't suppose I will, really," Marvin said. "And yet, what can I do? I have no body, and hosts are expensive."

"Too true. But did you ever fink of the Open Market? Eh?"

"But that's supposed to be dangerous," Marvin said, and blushed at the absurdity of his statement. The Erlan grinned toughly.

"Got the picture, eh, lad? But listen, it ain't so bad as you fink, long as you buck up and take aholt. Open Market's not so bad; been a lot of rot talked about it, mostly by the big Swap agencies that wanna go on charging their overinflated capitalistic damned fees. But I know a bloke been working there twenty years on Short Shuffles, and he tells me most of the blokes is straight as a die. So keep your head up and your chest prop tucked in tight, and pick yourself a good interman. Good luck, kid."

"Wait a moment!" Flynn cried, as the Erlan folded to his feet. "What is your friend's name?"

"James Virtue McHonnery," the Erlan said. "He's a tough, hard-bitten, narrow-minded little cuss, and over-fond of looking upon the grape when it is red, and inclined to be smitten by black rage when in his cups. But

45

he deals flat and he serves straight, and you couldn't ask no more than that from St. Xal himself. Just tell him that Pengle the Squib sent you, and good luck to you."

Flynn thanked the Squib eagerly, embarrassing that tough yet good-hearted gentleman. Rising to his feet, he proceeded, slowly at first, then with more speed, toward the Quain, in the northwest corner of which lay the many stalls and open booths of the Open Market. And his hopes, previously near entropy, began now to pulse modestly yet firmly. And in the nearby gutter, tattered newspapers flowed on a stream of sand toward the eternal and enigmatic desert.

"Hey-ya! Hey-ya! New bodies for old! Come and be serviced—new bodies for old!"

Marvin trembled when he heard that ancient street cry, so innocent in itself, yet so reminiscent of certain dark bedtime stories. Hesitantly he advanced into the tangled labyrinth of streets and alleys, or dead-ends and courtyards, that made up the ancient Free Market Area. And as he walked, a dozen shouted propositions assailed his aural receptors.

"Harvesters wanted to harvest the crop on Drogheda! We supply you with a fully functional body, complete with telepathy! All found, fifty credits a month, *and* a complete list of Class C-3 pleasures! Special two-year contracts are now being let. Come harvest the crop on beautiful Drogheda!"

"Serve in the Naigwin Army! Twenty NCO bodies currently on offer, plus a few specials in junior officer ranks. All bodies fully equipped with martial skills!"

"What's the pay?" a man asked the salesman.

46

"Your keep, plus one credit a month."

The man sneered and turned away.

"*And*," the barker proclaimed, "unlimited sacking rights."

"Well, that seems in order," the man said grudgingly. "But the Naigwins been losing this war for a decade. High casualty rate, and not much corporeal reclamation."

"We're changing all that," the salesman said. "You're an experienced mercenary?"

"Correct," the man said. "The name is Sean Von Ardin, and I've been in just about every major war around, plus a fair number of minor ones."

"Last rank?"

"Jevaldher in the army of the Count of Ganymede," Von Ardin said. "But before that I held the rank of Full Cthusis."

"Well, well," the salesman said, seemingly impressed. "Full Cthusis, eh? Got papers to prove it? OK, tell you what I can do. I can offer you a position with the Naigwins as Manatee Leader, Second Class."

Von Ardin frowned and calculated on his fingers. "Let's see, Manatee Leader Second Class is the equivalent of a Cyclopian Demi-Vale, which is slightly lower than an Anaxorean Banner King, and almost half a grade lower than a Dorian Old Boy. Which means . . . Hey, I'd lose an entire field grade if I joined you!"

"Ah, but you didn't hear me out," the salesman continued. "You would hold that rank for a period of 25 days, to prove Purity of Intent, which the Naigwin political leaders are very big on. *Then* we would jump you three entire grades to Melanoan Superios, which would

47

offer you an excellent chance at provisional Lance-Jumbaya, and maybe—I can't promise this, but I think I can swing it unofficially—*maybe* I can get you appointed Sackmeister for the spoils of Eridsvurg."

"Well," Von Ardin said, impressed in spite of himself, "that's a pretty decent deal—if you can swing it."

"Come into the store," the salesman said. "Let me make a phone call. . . ."

Marvin walked on and listened to men of a dozen races arguing with salesmen of a dozen more. A hundred propositions were screamed in his ear. His spirits were stirred and uplifted by the vitality of the place. And the propositions he heard, though sometimes dismaying, were often intriguing:

"Aphid-man wanted for the Senthis Swarm. Good pay, congenial friendships!"

"Rewrite man required to work on the *Dirty Book of Kavengii*! Must be able to empathize with sexual premises of the Midridarian race!"

"Garden planners needed for Arcturus! Come and relax among the only vegetable-sentients in the galaxy!"

"Expert manacler wanted for Vega IV! Opportunities also for semiskilled restrainers! Full prerogatives!"

There were so many opportunities in the galaxy! It seemed to Marvin that his misfortune was perhaps a blessing in disguise. He had wanted to travel—but his modesty had permitted him no more than the role of tourist. But how much better, how much more gratifying it would be, to travel for a reason: to serve with the armies of Naigwin, experience life as an aphid-man, learn what it meant to be a manacler—even to do rewrites on the *Dirty Book of Kavengii*.

48

Directly ahead of him, he spotted a sign that read: "James Virtue McHonnery, Licensed Short-Shuffle Dealer. Satisfaction guaranteed."

Standing at the waist-high counter and smoking a cigar was a tough, hard-bitten, sour-mouthed little man with piercing cobalt-blue eyes. This could be none other than McHonnery himself. Silent and disdainful, scorning to spiel, the little man stood with arms folded as Flynn walked up to the booth.

CHAPTER 8

THEY STOOD FACE TO FACE, FLYNN SLACK-
jawed, McHonnery clam-mouthed. Several seconds of
silence ensued. Then McHonnery said: "Look, kid, this
ain't no goddamned peep show and I ain't no goddamned
freak. If you got something to say, spit it out. Otherwise
take a walk for yourself before I break your back."

Marvin could see at once that this man was no fawn-
ing, honey-mouthed body salesman. There was no hint of
obsequiousness in that rasping voice, no trace of ingratia-
tion in that down-turned mouth. Here was a man who
said what he wanted to say, and took no heed of the
consequences.

"I—I am a client," Flynn said.

"Big deal," McHonnery harshed. "Am I supposed to
turn handsprings or something?"

His sardonic retort and blunt, inner-directed demeanor
gave Flynn a sensation of confidence. He knew, of
course, that appearances could be deceiving; but no one

51

had ever told him what to judge by instead of appearances. He was inclined to trust this proud and bitter man.

"I am going to be dispossessed of this body in a matter of hours," Marvin explained. "Since my own body has been stolen, I am in desperate need of a substitute. I have very little money, but I—I am quite willing and prepared to work."

McHonnery stared at him, and a sardonic grin twisted the man's tight lips. "Prepared to work, huh? Ain't that nice! And just what are you prepared to work *at*?"

"Why—anything."

"Yeah? Can you operate a Montcalm metal lathe with light-sensitive switchboard and manual cull? No? Think you could handle a Quick-Greeze Particle Separator for the Rare Earths Novelty Company? Not your sort of thing, huh? . . . I got a surgeon on Vega who wants somebody to run his Nerve-Impulse-Rejection Simulator (the old model with the double pedals). Not exactly what you had in mind? Well, we got a jazz band on Potemkin II which needs a stomach-horn man, and a restaurant near Boötes which could use a short-order cook, with working knowledge of Cthensis specialties. Doesn't ring a bell? Maybe you could pick flowers on Moriglia; of course, you'd have to be able to predict anthesis without more than a five-second variation. Or you could do spot-flesh-welding, if you've got the nerves for it, or boss a phylopod reclamation project, or draw up intermediate creeper systems, or—but I don't guess none of them strike your fancy, huh?"

Flynn shook his head and mumbled, "I don't know anything about any of those jobs, sir."

"Somehow," McHonnery said, "that doesn't surprise me as much as you might think. Is there anything you *can* do?"

"Well, in college I was studying—"

"Don't give me your goddamned life story! I'm interested in your trade, skill, talent, profession, ability, whatever you want to call it. What, specifically, can you *do?*"

"Well," Marvin said, "I guess when you put it that way, I can't do anything much."

"I know," McHonnery said, sighing. "You're unskilled; it's written all over you. Kid, it may interest you to know that unskilled minds are common as dirt, commoner. The market's glutted with them, the universe is crammed to overflowing with them. It may interest you to know that there is nothing you can do that a machine can't do better, faster, and a damn sight more cheerfully."

"I'm sorry to hear that, sir," Marvin said, sadly but with dignity. He turned to go.

"Just a minute," McHonnery said. "I thought you wanted to work."

"But you said—"

"I said you were unskilled, which you are. And I said that a machine can do anything you can do better, faster, and more cheerfully, *but not more cheaply.*"

"Oh," Marvin said.

"Yep, in the cheapness department, you still got an edge over the gadgets. And that's quite an achievement in this day and age. I have always considered it one of the glories of mankind that, despite its best efforts, it has never completely succeeded in rendering itself superfluous. You see, kid, our instincts order us to multiply, while our intelligence commands us to conserve. We are like a

53

father who bears many sons, but contrives to dispossess all but the eldest. We call instinct blind, but intelligence is equally so. Intelligence has its passions, its loves and its hates; woe to the logician whose superbly rational system does not rest upon a solid base of raw feeling. Lacking such a base, we call that man—irrational!"

"I never knew that," Marvin said.

"Well, hell, it's obvious enough," McHonnery said. "The aim of intelligence is to put the whole goddamned human race out of work. Luckily, it can never be done. A man will outwork a machine any day in the week. In the brute-labor department, there'll always be opportunities for the unwanted."

"I suppose there's a certain comfort in that," Flynn said doubtfully. "And of course, it's very interesting. But when Pengle the Squib told me to go see you, I thought—"

"Hey, how's that?" McHonnery said. "You're a friend of the Squib?"

"You might say that," Flynn said, thus avoiding an outright lie, since anyone might say anything whether it was true or not.

"You should have told me that in the first place," McHonnery said. "Not that it would have changed anything, since the facts are exactly as I have stated them. But I'd have told you that there's no shame in being unskilled; hell, all of us have to start out that way, don't we? If you do well on a Short-Shuffle contract, you'll pick up skills in no time."

"I hope so, sir," Flynn said, growing cautious now that McHonnery had become affable. "Do you have a job in mind for me?"

"As a matter of fact, I do," McHonnery said. It's a one-week Shuffle, which, even if you don't like it, you could do standing on your head. Not that you should have to, since it's a pleasant and compatible job, combining mild outdoor exercise with modest intellectual stimulation, all in a framework of good working conditions, an enlightened management, and a congenial working force."

"It sounds marvellous," Flynn said. "What's wrong with it?"

"Well, it's not the sort of job you can get rich at," McHonnery said. "In fact, the pay is lousy. But what the hell, you can't have everything. A week at this will give you a chance to think things over, talk with your fellow workers, decide upon a direction for yourself."

"What is the job?" Marvin asked.

"The official job title is Ootheca Indagator, Second Class."

"That sounds impressive."

"Glad that you like it. It means that you hunt for eggs."

"Eggs?"

"Eggs. Or to be more specific, you hunt for and, upon finding, collect, the eggs of the rock ganzer. Think you can swing it?"

"Well, I'd like to know a little more about the techniques utilized for the collecting, and also about job conditions, and—"

He stopped because McHonnery was slowly, sadly shaking his head. "You can find that out when you get there. I ain't delivering no goddamned travelogue, and you ain't deciding on no guided tour. Do you want the job or not?"

"Do you have anything else available?"

"No."

"Then I'll take the job."

"You've made a smart decision," McHonnery said. He took a paper out of his pocket. "Here is the standard government-approved contract, written in Kro-Melden, which is the official language of the planet Melde II, wherein is licensed the employing company. Can you read Kro-Melden?"

"I'm afraid not."

"Then I'll translate the pertinent clauses for you, as required by law. Let's see . . . standard stuff about the Company not being responsible for fire, earthquake, atomic warfare, sun going nova, acts of god or gods, and so forth. The Company agrees to hire you for the sum of one credit a month, plus transportation to Melde; there it will furnish you with a Melde body; it will further issue you a set of clothes, and will feed and shelter you and care for your health and welfare, unless it finds itself unable to do so, in which case it won't and you will hold it harmless for that failure. In return for these and other Services, you will perform designated tasks as instructed, in this case those tasks exclusively relating to and specifically effecting upon the finding and collecting of ganzer eggs. And may God have mercy on your soul."

"I beg your pardon?" Flynn asked.

"The last is just the standard invocation. Let me see, I think that about covers it. You guarantee, of course, not to commit acts of sabotage, espionage, irreverence, disobedience, etc., and to furthermore eschew and desist from the practices of sexual perversion as defined in Hoffmeyer's *Standard Book of Melden Perversions*. And you also guarantee not to initiate a war, or to take part in a war on Melde if one is initiated, and to wash once every two days, and to stay out of debt, and not to become an alcoholic or insane person, and various other things to which no reasonable person could possibly object. And that about sums it up. If you have any important questions, I'll endeavor to answer them for you."

"Well," Flynn said, "about those things I'm supposed to guarantee—"

"That's unimportant," McHonnery said. "Do you want the job or not? A simple yes or no will suffice."

Marvin had his doubts, but, unfortunately, he didn't have any alternatives; and this lack rendered his doubts extraneous to the situation. He thought fleetingly of the detective, then he put that thought firmly aside. As McHonnery had said, how bad could a week of anything be? Therefore he agreed to take the job, registering his assent upon the mind-sensitive universal signaturizer at the bottom of the page. McHonnery led him forthwith to the Transportation Center, from which point minds were shipped across the galaxy at a multiple of the speed of thought.

The next thing Marvin knew, he was on Melde, in a Melden body.

CHAPTER 9

THE GANZER RAIN FOREST ON MELDE WAS
deep and wide; the faintest ghost of a breeze whispered
among the colossal trees, slithered through the interlocked
vines, and crept broken-backed over hook-edged grass.
Drops of water slid painfully down and around the
tangled foliage like exhausted runners of a maze, coming
to rest at last in the spongy and indifferent soil.
Shadows mingled and danced, faded and reappeared,
called into spurious motion by two tired suns in a
moldy green sky. Overhead, a desolate therengol whistled for his mate, and heard in reply the quick ominous
cough of a predatory kingspringer. And through this
dolorous woodland, so tantalizingly like Earth and yet so
different, Marvin Flynn moved in his unfamiliar Melden
body, his eyes downcast, searching for ganzer eggs but
not knowing what they looked like.

All had been haste. From the moment he arrived on
Melde, he had barely had a chance to take stock of him-

59

self. No sooner was he bodified than someone was barking orders in his ear. Flynn had just had time to look hastily over his four-armed, four-legged body, give his tail a single experimental flick, and fold his ears across his back; then he was herded into a work gang, given a barracks number and a mess-hall location, and handed a jumper two sizes too big for him, and shoes that fitted tolerably well except for the left front. He signed for and was given the tools of his new trade; a large plastic bag, dark glasses, a compass, a net, a pair of tongs, a heavy metal tripod, and a blaster.

He and his fellow workers were then assembled in ranks, and received a hasty indocrination lecture by the manager, a bored and supercilious Atreian.

Flynn learned that his new home occupied an insignificant portion of space in the vicinity of Aldeberan. Melde (so named for its dominant race, the Meldens) was a thoroughly second-rate world. Its climate was rated "intolerable" on the Hurlihan-Chanz Climatic Tolerance Scale; its natural-resource potentiality was classified "submarginal," and its esthetic-resonance factor (unweighted) was given as "unprepossessing."

"Not the sort of place," the manager said, "that one would choose for a vacation, or indeed, for anything, except possibly the practice of extreme mortification."

His audience tittered uneasily.

"Nevertheless," the manager continued, "this unloved and unlovely place, this solar misfortune, this cosmic mediocrity is home to its inhabitants, who consider it the finest place in the universe."

The Meldens, with a fierce pride in their only tangible asset, had made the best of their bad bargain. With the

60

plucky determination of the eternally unlucky, they had farmed the edges of the rain forest and collected meagre low-yield ores from the vast blazing deserts. Their dogged persistence would have been inspiring had it not been so tedious; and their efforts might have been considered a tribute to the vaunting spirit of life had they not invariably ended in failure. Because, despite all their travail, the Meldens were able to achieve nothing better than slow starvation in the present, and the promise of racial degeneration and extinction in the future.

"This, then, is Melde," said the manager. "Or rather, this is *what Melde would be* were it not for one additional factor. That factor spells the difference between success and failure. I refer, of course, to the presence of ganzer eggs."

"Ganzer eggs!" the manager repeated. "No other planet possesses them; no other planet so desperately needs them. Ganzer eggs! No object in the known universe so clearly epitomizes the quality of desirability. Ganzer eggs! Let us consider them, if you will."

Ganzer eggs were the sole export of the planet Melde. And luckily for the Meldens, the eggs were always in heavy use. On Orichades, ganzer eggs were utilized as love-objects; on Opiuchus II, they were ground up and eaten as a sovereign aphrodisiac; on Morichades, after consecration, they were worshipped by the irrational K'tengi. Many other uses could be cited.

Thus, ganzer eggs were a vital natural resource, and the only one which the Meldens possessed. With them, the Meldens could maintain a tolerable degree of civilization. Without them, the race would surely perish.

To acquire a ganzer egg, all one had to do was pick it

up. But therein lay certain difficulties, since the ganzers, not unnaturally, objected to this practice.

The ganzers were forest dwellers, remotely of lizard origin. They also were destroyers, clever at concealment, wily and ferocious, and completely untamable. These qualities rendered the collection of ganzer eggs extremely perilous.

"It is a curious situation," the manager pointed out, "and not without its paradoxical overtones, that the main source of life on Melde is also the main cause of death. It is something for you all to think about as you begin your workday. And so I say, take good care of yourselves, keep guarded at all times, look before you leap, observe every precaution with your indentured lives, and also with the costly bodies which have been entrusted to your keeping. But in addition, remember that you must fulfill your norm, since every day's work unfulfilled by so much as a single egg is penalized by the addition of an additional week. Therefore, be careful, but not too careful, and be perseverant, but not blindly so, and courageous, but not rash, and assiduous, but never foolhardy. Follow these simple maxims and you will have no difficulty. Good luck, boys!"

Marvin and his fellow workers were then formed into ranks and marched into the forest on the double.

Within an hour they reached their search area. Marvin Flynn took this opportunity to ask the foreman for instructions.

"Instructions?" the foreman asked. "What kind of type instructions?" (He was an Orinathian deportee with no language aptitude.)

"I mean," Flynn said, "what am I supposed to do?"

The foreman pondered the question and at length responded: "You supposed pick eggs of ganzer." (Amusingly enough, he pronounced it "guntser.")

"I understand that," Flynn said. "But I mean to say, I don't even know what a ganzer egg looks like."

"Not to worry," the foreman replied. "You know when see no mistake, yes."

"Yes, sir," Marvin said "And when I find a ganzer egg, are there any special rules for handling it? I mean to say, is breakage a problem, or—"

"To handle," the foreman said, "you pick up egg, put in bag. You understand this thing yes no?"

"Of course I do," Marvin said. "But also, I would like to know about daily-quota expectations. I mean to say, is there some sort of a quota system, or perhaps an hourly breakdown? I mean, how does one know when one has fulfilled his norm?"

"Ah!" said the foreman, a look of comprehension finally crossing his broad, good-natured face. "Of finish is like this. You pick ganzer egg, put in bag, check?"

"Check," Marvin said instantly.

"You do so time after time *until bag is full*. Catch?"

"I believe I do," Marvin said. "The full bag represents the actual or ideal quota. Let me just go over the steps again to make absolutely sure I've got it. First, I locate the ganzer eggs, applying Terran associations to the concept, and presumably having no difficulty in identification. Second, having located and identified the desired object, I proceed to 'put it in my basket,' by which I assume that I lift it manually to initiate the transaction, and then proceed with actions consonant with that beginning. Third, repeating this strategy S for an x number of times, I perform the equation $Sx=B!$, when B represents the capacity of the bag and $!$ represents the sum of x transactions necessary to fulfill B. Finally, the sum of all strategies completed, I return to the camp, where I turn in the contents of my bag. Do I have it straight, sir?"

The foreman tapped his teeth with his tail and said, "You put me on, huh, kid?"

"Well, sir, I merely wished to ascertain—"

"You make big joke on old-planet Orinathian yokel, yah, sure, huh. You think you so smart, but you ain't so smart. Remember—nobody likes wise guy."

"I'm sorry," Flynn said, swishing his tail deferentially. (But he wasn't sorry. It was his first show of spirit since this downward-trending series of events had begun for him, and he was glad to find himself capable of some show of spirit, no matter how ill-timed or badly considered.)

"Anyhow, me I tink you catch elementary rudiments of job all right so you go now perform work-labor *big*, and keep nose clean or I break six or more of your limbs, dig?"

"Dig," said Flynn, wheeled and cantered into the forest and there began his search for ganzer eggs.

CHAPTER 10

MARVIN FLYNN WONDERED AS HE WAN-
dered just what a ganzer egg looked like. He also would
have enjoyed knowing what he was supposed to use his
equipment for; the sunglasses were useless in the dim re-
cesses of the forest, and the heavy tripod was incompre-
hensible.

He slid silently through the forest, his nostrils flared
wide, his eyes extended and swiveling, their blink-rate
reduced. His golden hide, scented faintly with appis-
thyme, twitched sensitively as his great muscles moved
beneath it, apparently relaxed yet poised for instant action.

The forest was a symphony of greens and grays, cut
through with the occasional scarlet theme of a creeper,
or the purple flourish of a lillibabba shrub, or rarer still,
the haunting oboe countermelody of an orange whip-
whinger. Yet withal, the effect was essentially a somber

65

and thought-provoking one, like the sight of a vast amusement park in the silent hour before dawn.

But there! Right over there! A little to the left! Yes, yes, just beneath the boku tree! Is that . . . ? Could it be . . . ?

Flynn parted the leaves with his right arms and bent low. There, in a nest of grass and woven twigs, he saw a glittering ovoid that resembled nothing quite so much as an ostrich egg encrusted with precious gems.

The foreman had been right. There could be no mistaking a ganzer egg.

Gazing carefully upon that singular object, and taking stock of his impressions, Marvin could see the light of a million fairy fires burning bright in the curved and multihued ganzer surface. Shadows drifted across it like the fragrance of half-remembered dreams, twisting and turning like the descending ghosts of phantoms. An emotion welled up in Marvin, of twilight and evensong, of slow cattle grazing near a crystal brook, of dusty, heartbroken cypresses beside a white stone road.

Although it wrenched his sensibilities to do so, Marvin bent down and reached out, with the straightforward intention of lifting the ganzer egg and sequestering it within his plastic bag. His hand folded lovingly around the glowing orb.

He pulled his hand back quickly; the glowing orb was hotter than hell.

Marvin looked at the ganzer egg with new respect. Now he understood the purpose of the tongs with which he had been equipped. He maneuvered them into position and closed the jaws gently on the spheroid of dreams.

66

The spheroid of dreams bounced away from him like a rubber ball. Marvin galloped after it, fumbling with his net. The ganzer egg twisted and ricocheted, and bolted for thick underbrush. Marvin cast his net in desperation, and fortune guided his hand. The ganzer egg was neatly netted. It lay quietly, pulsating as though out of breath. Marvin approached it cautiously, ready for any trick.

Instead, the ganzer egg spoke. "Look, mister," it said, in a muffled voice. "Just what's eating you?"

"Beg pardon?" Marvin said.

"Look," the ganzer egg said, "I am sitting here in a public park minding my own business when suddenly you come up and pounce on me like a lunatic, bruising my shoulder and acting in general like some kind of nut. Well, naturally, I get a little hot. Who wouldn't? So I decide to move away because it's my day off and I don't want no trouble. So you up and throw a net around me like I was a goddamned *fish* or a butterfly or something. So I just want to know, what's the big idea?"

"Well," Marvin said, "you see, you're a ganzer egg."

"I'm aware of that," the ganzer egg said. "Sure I'm a ganzer egg. Is there a law against that all of a sudden?"

"Certainly not," Marvin said. "But as it happens, I am hunting ganzer eggs."

There was a short silence. Then the ganzer egg said, "Would you mind repeating that?"

Marvin did. The ganzer egg said, "Mmm, that's what I thought you said." He laughed feebly. "You're kidding, aren't you?"

"Sorry, I'm not."

"Sure you are," the ganzer egg said, a note of desperation in his voice. "So OK, you've had your fun. Now let me out of here."

"Sorry . . ."

"*Let me out!*"

"I can't."

"Why?"

"Because I'm hunting ganzer eggs."

"My God," the ganzer egg said, "this is the craziest thing I've ever heard in my life. You never met me before, did you? So why are you hunting me?"

"I've been hired to hunt ganzer eggs," Marvin told him.

"Look, fella, are you trying to tell me that you just go around hunting any ganzer egg at all? You don't care which one?"

"That's right."

"And you aren't really looking for one *particular* ganzer egg who maybe did you a bad turn?"

"No, no," Marvin said. "I've never even met a ganzer egg before."

"You've never . . . and yet you hunt . . . ? I must be going out of my mind, I can't be hearing right. I mean, things like this just don't happen. I mean, it's like some kind of an incredible nightmare . . . . I mean, it's the sort of thing you get crazy nightmares about—some crazy-looking guy walking up calm as you please and grabbing you and saying in a sort of crazy dead-pan voice, 'I happen to be hunting for ganzer eggs.' I mean—look, fella, you *are* putting me on, aren't you?"

Marvin was embarrassed and exasperated, and he wished the ganzer egg would shut up. He said gruffly, "I'm not fooling. My job is to collect ganzer eggs."

"Collect . . . ganzer eggs!" the ganzer egg moaned. "Oh

no, no, no, no! My God, I can't believe this is happening, and yet it really is happening, it really is—"

"Control yourself," Marvin said; the ganzer egg was clearly on the thin edge of hysteria.

"Thank you," the ganzer egg said, after a moment. "I'm all right now. I didn't mean to—to give way."

"That's all right," Marvin said. "Are you ready to be collected now?"

"I—I'm trying to get used to the idea. It's so . . . so . . . Look, could I ask you just one question?"

"Hurry it up," Marvin said.

"The thing I want to ask," the ganzer egg said, "do you get some kind of a charge out of this sort of thing? I mean are you some sort of pervert? I don't mean to be insulting."

"That's all right," Marvin said. "No, I'm not a pervert, and I can assure you I take no pleasure in this. It's strictly a job with me."

"Strictly a job," the ganzer egg repeated. "A *job*. To kidnap a ganzer egg whom you've never met before. Just a job. Like picking up a stone. Only I'm not a stone, I'm a ganzer egg!"

"I realize that," Marvin said. "Believe me, I'm finding all of this very strange."

"*You're* finding it strange!" the ganzer egg said, his voice rising to a scream. "How do you think I feel? Do you think maybe I think it's *natural* for someone to come along like in a nightmare and *collect* me?"

"Steady," Marvin said.

"Sorry," the ganzer egg said. "I'm all right now."

"I'm really very sorry about this," Marvin said. "But

you see, I've got this job and this quota, and if I don't do it I'll have to spend the rest of my life here."

"Crazy," the ganzer egg whispered to himself. "He's absolutely and completely insane."

"So I have to collect you," Marvin finished, and reached out.

"Wait!" the ganzer egg howled, in so panic-stricken a voice that Marvin desisted.

"What is it now?"

"May—may I leave a note for my wife?"

"There isn't time," Marvin said firmly.

"Then will you at least let me say my prayers?"

"Go ahead and say them," Marvin said. "But you'll really have to be quick about it."

"Oh Lord God," the ganzer egg intoned, "I don't know what is happening to me, or why. I have always tried to be a good person, and although I am not a regular churchgoer, You surely know that true religion is in the heart. I've maybe done some bad things in my life, I won't deny it. But Lord, why this punishment? Why me? Why not someone else, one of the real bad ones, one of the criminals? Why me? And why like this? Something is *collecting* me like I'm some sort of a *thing.* . . . And I don't understand. But I know that You are All-Wise and All-Powerful, and I know that You are good, so I guess there must be a reason . . . even if I'm too stupid to see it. So look, God, if this is it, then OK, this is it. But could you look after my wife and kids? And could you especially look after the little one?" The ganzer egg's voice broke, but he recovered almost at once. "I ask especially for the little one, God, because he's lame and the other kids pick on him and he needs a lot—a lot of love. Amen."

70

The ganzer egg choked back his sobs. His voice became abruptly stronger.

"All right," he said to Marvin. "I'm ready now. Go ahead and do your damnedest, you lousy son-of-a-bitch."

But the prayer of the ganzer egg had unmanned Marvin completely. With eyes wet and fetlocks trembling, Marvin opened the net and released his captive. The ganzer egg rolled out a little distance and then stopped, clearly fearing a trick.

"You—you really mean this?" he said.

"I do," Marvin said. "I was never cut out for this kind of work. I don't know what they will do to me back at the camp, but I shall never gather a single ganzer egg!"

"Praised be the name of the Lord," the ganzer egg said softly. "I've seen a few strange things in my time, but it seems to me that the Hand of Providence—"

The hypothesis of the ganzer egg (known as the Interventionalist Fallacy) was interrupted by a sudden ominous crashing in the underbrush. Marvin whirled, and remembered the dangers of the planet Melde. He had been warned, but had forgotten. And now, desperately, he fumbled for his blaster, which had become entangled in his net. Violently he wrenched at it, pulled it free, heard a shrill warning from the ganzer egg—

And then he was flung violently to the ground. The blaster spun away into the underbrush. And Marvin gazed up into slit black eyes beneath a low armored forehead.

No introductions were necessary. Flynn knew that he had met a full-grown adult marauding ganzer, and had met him under possibly the worst of all circumstances.

The evidence (if evidence were needed) was all too evident; close to hand was the damning net, the telltale sunglasses, the revealing tongs. And closer still—closing on his neck—was the tooth-edged jaw of the gigantic saurian, so close that Marvin could see three gold molars and a temporary porcelain filling.

Flynn tried to wriggle free. The ganzer pressed him back with a paw the size of a yak saddle; his cruel claws, each the size of a pair of ice tongs, bit cruelly into Marvin's golden hide. The slavering jaws gaped hideously, descended, about to engulf his entire head. . . .

CHAPTER 11

SUDDENLY—TIME STOPPED! MARVIN SAW the ganzer's jaws arrested in midslaver, his bloodshot left eye fixed in midblink, and his entire great body gripped in a strange and unyielding rigidity.

Nearby, the ganzer egg was as motionless as a carven replica of itself.

The breeze was stopped in midcareer. Trees were caught in straining postures, and a meritheian hawk was fixated in midflight like a dummy attached to a wire.

The sun stopped its inexorable rolling flight!

And in this strange tableau, Marvin stared with tremulous sensations in the direction of a single movement in the air three feet above his head and slightly to his left.

It began as a whorl of dust, broadened, expanded, expatiated, thickening at the base and becoming convex at the apex. The rotation came faster, and the figure solidified.

"Detective Urdorf!" Marvin cried. For it was indeed

the Martian detective with the streak of bad luck who had promised to solve Marvin's case and to return to him his rightful body.

"Terribly sorry to barge in like this," Urdorf said, materializing fully and falling heavily to the ground.

"Thank God you have come!" Marvin said. "You have saved me from an extremely unpleasant fate, and now if you will help me out from under this creature—"

For Marvin was still pinned to the ground by the ganzer's paw, which had taken on the rigidity of tempered steel, and from beneath which he was unable to wriggle.

"Sorry," the detective said, getting up and dusting himself off. "I'm afraid I can't do that."

"Why not?"

"Because it's against the rules," Detective Urdorf told him. "You see, any displacement of bodies during an artificial induced temporal stoppage (which is what this is) could result in a Paradox, which is forbidden since it might result in a temporal implosion which might conceivably have the result of warping the structure-lines of our continuum and thus destroy the universe. Because of this, any displacement is punishable by a prison sentence of one year and a fine of one thousand credits."

"Oh. I didn't know that," Marvin said.

"Well, I'm afraid that's how it is," the detective said.

"I see," Marvin said.

"I rather hoped you would," the detective said.

There was a long and uncomfortable silence. Then Marvin said, "Well?"

"Beg pardon?"

"I said—I *meant* to say, Why did you come here?"

74

"Oh," the detective said. "I wished to ask you several questions which had not occurred to me earlier, and which would assist me in the rigorous investigation and solution of this case."

"Ask away," Marvin said.

"Thank you. First and foremost, what is your favorite color?"

"Blue."

"But exactly what *shade* of blue? Please try to be exact."

"Robin's-egg blue."

"Hmmm." The detective noted it down in his notebook. "And now, tell me quickly and without thinking, what is the first number that comes into your mind?"

"87792.3," Marvin replied without hesitation.

"Um hum. And now, without reflection, tell me the name of the first popular song you can think of."

" 'Orang-Utan Rhapsody,' " Marvin said.

"Ummmm. Fine," Urdorf said, snapping his notebook shut. "I think that covers everything."

"What was the purpose of those questions?" Marvin asked.

"With this information, I will be able to test various suspects for corpus-vestigial responses. It is part of the Duulman self-identity quiz."

"Oh," Marvin said. "Have you had any luck yet?"

"Luck hardly enters into it," Urdorf replied. "But I can say that the case is proceeding in a satisfactory manner. We traced the thief to Iorama II, where he smuggled himself into a cargoload of flash-frozen beef destined for Goera Major. On Goera he represented himself as a fugitive from Hage XI, which won him a good deal of popular favor. He managed to raise enough money for fare to Kvanthis, where he had cached his money. Staying no more than a day on Kvanthis, he boarded the local to the Fiftystars Autonomous Region."

"And then?" Marvin asked.

"Then we lost track of him temporarily. Fiftystars Region contains no less than 432 planetary systems with a combined population of 300 billion. So as you can see, our work is cut out for us."

"It sounds hopeless," Marvin said.

"Quite the contrary, it is a very good break for us. Laymen always mistake complication for complexity. But our criminal will find no safety in mere multiplicity, which is always susceptible to statistical analysis."

"So what happens now?" Marvin asked.

"We continue analyzing, and then we make a projection based upon the probabilities, and then we send our projection across the galaxy and see if it goes nova. . . . I am speaking figuratively, of course."

"Of course," Marvin said. "Do you really think you'll catch him?"

"I am fully confident of the results," Detective Urdorf said. "But you must have patience. You must remember that intergalactic crime is still a relatively new field, and therefore intergalactic investigation is newer still. There have been many crimes in which even the existence of a criminal could not be proven, much less detected. So in some respects, we are ahead of the game."

"I guess I'll have to take your word for it," Marvin said.

"Just don't worry. In these cases, it is best for the victim to continue his life as normally as possible, to stay

76

alive, and not to give way to despair. I hope you will remember this."

"I'll try to," Marvin said. "But about this situation I'm in at present—"

"It is the very sort of situation I have told you to avoid," the detective said severely. "Please remember that in the future, if you should manage to come out of this alive. Good luck, my friend, and stay alive!"

Before Marvin's eyes, detective Urdorf revolved, faster, faster, grew dimmer, and disappeared.

Time unfroze.

And Marvin gazed up again into the ganzer's slit black eyes and low armored forehead, and saw the hideous gaping jaws descending, about to engulf his entire head. . . .

CHAPTER 12

"WAIT!" MARVIN SHOUTED.

"What for?" the ganzer asked.

Marvin hadn't thought that far. He heard the ganzer egg muttering, "Turnabout's fair play; and yet, he was kind to me. Still, what business is it of mine? Stick your neck out, somebody cracks your shell. And yet . . ."

"I don't want to die," Marvin said.

"I didn't suppose you did," the rock ganzer said, in a not unfriendly voice. "And, of course, you want to discuss it with me. Ethics, morals, the whole bit. But I'm afraid not. We were specifically warned, you see, never to allow a Melden to talk. We were told to just do the job and get it over with, not to *personalize* it. Just do it and get on to the next bit of work. Mental hygiene, really. Therefore, if you would close your eyes . . ."

The jaws moved closer. But Marvin, filled with wild surmise, cried out: "Did you say *job?*"

"Of course, it's a job," the ganzer said. "There's nothing personal in it." He frowned, apparently annoyed at himself for having spoken.

"A job! Your job is to hunt Meldens, is that it?"

"Well, obviously. This planet of Ganzer isn't good for much, you see, except for hunting Meldens."

"But why do you hunt them?" Marvin asked.

"Well, for one thing, a ganzer egg can grow to full maturity only in the host-flesh of the adult Melden."

"I *say*," the ganzer egg said, rolling around with embarrassment, "must we get so damned *biological*? I mean to say, you don't hear me talking about *your* natural functions, do you?"

"And secondly," the ganzer continued, "our sole export is Melden hides, which (after curing and tanning) are used for imperial vestments on Triana II, for good-luck charms on Nemo, and for seat covers on Chrysler XXX. This quest for the elusive and deadly Melden is our sole means of maintaining a tolerable degree of civilization, and—"

"That's exactly what they told me!" Marvin cried, and quickly repeated what the manager had said to him.

"My gosh!" said the ganzer.

Both realized the true situation now: the Meldens were utterly dependent upon the Ganzers, who in turn were utterly dependent upon the Meldens. These two races hunted each other, lived and died for each other, and, through ignorance or guile, ignored any relationship between each other. The relationship was utterly symbiotic, but completely unacknowledged by either race. In fact, each race pretended that it alone was a Civilized Intelligence, and that the other was bestial, contemptible, and of no account.

80

And it now occurred to both of them that they were, in equal measure, participants in the general concept of Humanity. (The ganzer egg was also a part, of course.)

The realization was awesome; but Marvin was still pinned to the ground by the ganzer's heavy paw.

"This leaves me in a somewhat embarrassing situation," the ganzer said, after a while. "My natural tendency is to release you; but I am working on this planet under a contract, which stipulates—"

"Then you are not a real ganzer?"

"No. I am a Swapper like yourself, and I come from Terra!"

"My home planet!" Marvin cried.

"I had guessed as much," the ganzer replied. "After a time one becomes sensitive to the idiosyncratic quality of differing minds, and learns to recognize one's countrymen through little tricks of thought and phraseology. I would guess that you are an American, probably from the East Coast, perhaps from Connecticut or Vermont—"

"New York State!" Marvin cried. "I am from Stanhope!"

"And I am from Saranac Lake," the ganzer said. "My name is Otis Dagobert, and I am thirty-seven years old."

And with that, the ganzer lifted his paw from Marvin's chest. "We are neighbors," he said quietly. "And so I cannot kill you, just as I am reasonably sure you would be unable to kill me, had you the opportunity. And now that we know the truth, I doubt if we will be able to perform any portion of our terrible jobs. But that is a sad thing to find out, for it means that we are doomed to Contractual Discipline; and then if we do not obey, our

Companies will give us Extreme Severance. And you know what that means."

Marvin nodded sadly. He knew all too well. His head drooped, and he sat in disconsolate silence beside his newly found friend.

"I can think of no way out," Marvin said, after giving the matter some thought. "Perhaps we could hide in the forest for a few days; but they would be sure to find us."

Suddenly, the ganzer egg spoke up. "Come now, perhaps it isn't as hopeless as you think!"

"What do you mean?" Marvin asked.

"Well now," the ganzer egg said, dimpling with pleasure, "it seems to me that one good turn deserves another. I could get into plenty of hot water for this. . . . But to hell with that. I think I can find a way off this planet for both of you."

Both Marvin and Otis broke into exclamations of gratitude; but the ganzer egg stopped them at once.

"Maybe you won't thank me when you see what lies ahead," he said ominously.

"Nothing could be worse than this," Otis said.

"You'd be surprised," the ganzer egg said flatly. "You might be very surprised. . . . This way, gentlemen."

"But where are we going?" Marvin asked.

"I'm taking you to meet the Hermit," the ganzer egg replied, and would say no more. He rolled purposefully away, and Marvin and Otis followed.

CHAPTER 13

THROUGH THE RAIN FOREST WILD AND free of Ganzer (or Melde, depending upon your point of view), they marched and rolled, ever alert for danger. But no creature menaced them, and they came at last to a clearing in the forest. They saw a rude hut in the center of that clearing, and a humanoform creature dressed all in rags, squatting in front of the hut.

"That is the Hermit," said the ganzer egg. "He's quite insane."

The two Terrans had no time in which to consider that information. The Hermit arose and cried, "Now stand, hold, halt! Reveal yourselves to my understanding!"

"I'm Marvin Flynn," Marvin said, "and this is my friend Otis Dagobert. We want to escape from this planet."

The Hermit didn't seem to hear them; he stroked his long beard and gazed thoughtfully at the treetops. In low somber tones, he said:

"Ere this moment came, a flight of geese
Passed low o'erhead, presaging woe;
The refuge and disconsolate owl did pass
This hid'n' place of mine, bereft
Of that which nature freely gives but man denies!
The stars are silent when they light our home:
The trees themselves proclaim the flight of kings."

"He means," the ganzer egg said, "that he had a feeling you'd be coming this way."

"Is he crazy or something?" Otis asked. "The way he talks—"

"Now rede me this! I'll have no plattering roth
To creep between the interstices of a mind
Proclaiming treason,"
the hermit said.

"He doesn't want you to whisper to each other," the ganzer egg translated. "It makes him suspicious."

"I could figure that much out for myself," Flynn said.

"So go screw yourself," the ganzer egg said. "I was just trying to be helpful."

The hermit advanced several paces, halted, and said: "What wot ye here aroon?"

Marvin looked at the ganzer egg, who remained obstinately silent. So, guessing at the meaning of the words, Marvin said, "Sir, we are trying to escape from this planet, and we have come to you for help."

The hermit shook his head and said,

"What barbrous tongue is this? A thick-mouthed sheep
Would clothe his meaning in a sound more clear!"

84

"What does he mean?" Marvin asked.

"You're so smart, figure it out for yourself," the ganzer egg said.

"I'm sorry if I insulted you," Marvin said.

"Forget it, forget it."

"I really am sorry. I'd appreciate it if you'd translate for us."

"All right," the ganzer egg said, still a little sulkily. "He says he doesn't understand you."

"He doesn't? But what I said to him was clear enough."

"Not to him," the ganzer egg said. "You want to reach him, you'd better put it in meter."

"Me? I couldn't!" Marvin said, with that instinctual shudder of revulsion which all intelligent Terran males feel at the thought of verse. "I simply couldn't! Otis, maybe you—"

"Not me!" Otis said, alarmed. "What do you think I am? A fag?"

"A silence swells and grows; yet honest men
Speak bold, with well-formed mouth! Melikes it not
What this development portends."

"He's getting edgy," the ganzer egg said. "You better have a shot at it."

"Perhaps you could do it for us," Otis suggested.

"I'm no fag," the ganzer egg sneered. "If you want to speak, you'll have to speak for yourselves."

"The only poem I can remember from school is the *Rubáiyát*," Marvin said.

"Well, go to it," the ganzer egg said.

Marvin thought, twitched, and nervously said:

85

"Behold! A pilgrim from the forest war
Of race 'gainst race, does humbly implore
Your aid and sustenance, and help and hope.
Can you this humble earnest plea ignore?"

"Very shaky," whispered the ganzer egg. "But not bad for a first attempt." (Otis was giggling, and Marvin clouted him with his tail.)

The hermit replied:

"Well spoken, stranger! You shall have this aid.
Nay, more! For when men meet, despite their divers
    forms,
They needs must succor each one to his own."

More quickly now, Marvin replied:

"I hoped, in this ancient planetoid with dreams displayed
Of sunrise splendors, sunsets disarrayed,
That one poor pilgrim who did pass this way
Might find escape from terrors he surveyed."

The Hermit said:

"Step forward then, my friend, my liege, my lord,
For all men are consistent to that state
Which life shall bring to them; the veriest slave
May someday be the king of yonder peer,
While this man here, this enemy by rote
Of graven custom, shall at hand
Be cup companion, if his speech be known!"

Marvin stepped forward, saying:

"Much thanks! Your doorway to the stars
Fits wise man and fool; yet still it bars

The Mute, who through his foolish tongue unused
Won't even get one half the way to Mars."

Otis, who had been restraining his giggles through all
this, now said: "Hey! Were you saying something about
me?"

"I certainly was," Marvin said. "You'd better start
versifying if you want to get out of here."

"Well, rats, you're doing it for both of us."

"Nope. The Hermit just said you have to speak for
yourself."

"My God, what'll I do?" Otis muttered. "I don't
know any poetry."

"You better think of something," the ganzer egg said.

"Well . . . all I can remember is a little Swinburne
which some goopey girl talked to me once. It's pretty
stupid stuff."

"Let's hear it," Marvin said.

Otis sweated and swotted, and at last intoned:

"When the spaceships of Earth are on distant planets,
The soul of a man, be he slender or tall,
Desires his home, for it pulls like ten magnets,
Filling his heart as great waves fill a hall.
And the great green sensation of gratitude
Is entranced by the welcoming attitude
Of a heroic Hermit, whose modulent mood
Is to rescue the spaceman and save him withal."

The hermit said:

"I find thee apt: 'Tis parlous to relate
In these lean times a halting tongue may work
Quick mischief 'pon its saddened owner-lord."

Marvin said:

> "Ah come, take Marvin Flynn away, and leave
> The Rest to wrangle! He would grieve
> To find his body torn and wounded; therefore now
> He'd like to go, whilst others stand and cheer."

The hermit said:

> "Away then, gentlemen! Hearts high,
> Feet firm in stirrups, head uplifted be . . ."

And so they proceeded in sing-song fashion to the hermit's hut, where they saw, hidden away under some sheets of bark, an illegal Mindsender, of an ancient and curious design. And Marvin learned that there was method in even the direst madness. For the hermit had been on this planet for less than a year, and already had made a considerable fortune by smuggling refugees to the less savory labor markets of the galaxy.

It was not ethical, but as the hermit put it:

> "Call you it dastardly, then, the tricks I play
> With this my engine? Sobeit! Nay, I'll not dispute
> The arid-abstract trueness of your plea.
> Yet think upon't; 'tis folly to refuse bad wine
> When chok't with desert thirst. Not so? Then why
> So harshly judge the salvor of your life?
> 'Tis damned ingratitude of most perversity—
> To slap the hand that plucked Death's grip from thee!"

CHAPTER 14

A SMALL AMOUNT OF TIME PASSED. A JOB
for Otis Dagobert had not been difficult to find. Despite
his protestations to the contrary, the young man showed
a small but very promising streak of sadism. Accordingly,
the Hermit had Swapped him into the mind of a dental
assistant on Prodenda IX. That planet, just to the left of
the South Ridge stars if you come by way of Procyon,
had been settled by a group of Terrans who felt strongly
about fluorine, despising this chemical group as though it
were the devil itself. On Prodenda IX they could live
fluorine-free, with the assistance of many dental archi-
tects, as they were called.

The ganzer egg wished Marvin the best of good fortune and rolled off into the forest.

"And now," the hermit said, "we come to the problem
of you. It seems to me, considering your personality quite
objectively, that you have a definite aptitude as a victim."

"Me?" Marvin asked.

"Yes, you," the hermit replied.

"A victim?"

"Definitely a victim."

"I'm not so sure," Marvin replied. He stated it that way out of politeness; actually, he was quite sure the hermit was wrong."

"Well, I'm sure," the hermit said. "And I dare say I've had more experience in job placement than you."

"I suppose you have. . . . I notice that you are no longer speaking in verse."

"Of course not," the hermit said. "Why should I?"

"Because earlier," Marvin said, "you had been speaking only in verse."

"But that was entirely different," the hermit said. "I was outside then. I had to protect myself."

"But what about now?"

"Now I am in my house and therefore quite safe. I have no need for the protective language of verse."

"Does verse really protect you outside?" Marvin asked.

"It certainly does. I have lived on this planet for over a year, hunted by two murderous races who would kill me on sight if they could find me. And in that time I have suffered no harm whatsoever. What do you think about that?"

"Well, it's very fine, of course. But how do you know it's your language that protects you?"

"I infer it," the hermit said. "It seems a reasonable enough assumption."

"Yes, sir," Marvin said. "But I don't quite see the relationship between your language and your safety."

"I'll be damned if I see it, either," the hermit said. "I

like to think of myself as a rational man, but the efficacy of verse is one thing that I am reluctantly forced to accept on faith. It *works;* what more can I say?"

"Have you ever thought of experimenting?" Marvin asked. "I mean, speaking outside *without* your language of verse? You might find you don't need it."

"So I might," the hermit replied. "And if you tried walking on the ocean bottom, you might find that you didn't need air."

"It's not really the same thing," Marvin said.

"It's exactly the same thing," the hermit told him. "All of us live by the employment of countless untested assumptions, the truth or falsehood of which we can determine only through the hazard of our lives. Since most of us value our lives more than the truth, we leave such drastic tests for the fanatics."

"I don't try to walk on water," Marvin said, "because I've seen men drown."

"And I," the hermit said, "do not speak a prose language outside because I have seen too many men killed while speaking it; but I have not seen one single verse-speaker killed."

"Well . . . to each his own."

"The acceptance of indeterminacy is the beginning of wisdom," the hermit quoted. "But we were talking about you and victimization. I repeat, you have an aptitude, which opens the possibility of an extremely interesting position for you."

"I am not interested," Marvin said. "What else do you have available?"

"Nothing else," the hermit said.

By a remarkable coincidence, Marvin heard at that

moment a great crashing and thundering in the under-brush outside, and deduced that it was either the Meldens or the Ganzers, or both, coming in pursuit of him.

"I accept the job," Marvin said. "But you're wrong."

He had the satisfaction of the last word; but the hermit had the satisfaction of the last deed. For, arranging his equipment and adjusting his dials, he closed the switch and sent Marvin off to his new career on the planet Celsus V.

CHAPTER 15

ON CELSUS V, THE GIVING AND RECEIVING OF gifts is a cultural imperative. To refuse a gift is unthinkable; the emotion it raises in a Celsian is comparable to the incest-dread of a Terran. Normally, this causes no trouble. Most gifts are white gifts, intended to express various shades of love, gratitude, tenderness, etc. But there are also gray gifts of warning, and black gifts of death.

Thus, a certain public official received a handsome snout ring from his constituents. It was imperiously designed for two weeks' wear. It was a splendid object, and it had only one flaw. It ticked.

A creature of another race might have flung it into the nearest ditch. But no Celsian in his right mind would do that. He wouldn't even have the ring examined. Celsians live by the motto: DO not look a gift in the teeth. Besides, if word of his suspicion leaked out, it would cause an irreparable public scandal.

He had to wear that damned ring for two weeks.

But the damn thing was *ticking*.

The official, whose name was Marduk Kras, pondered the problem. He thought about his constituents, and various ways he had helped them, and various other ways he had failed them. The ring was a warning, that much was clear. It was *at best* a warning—a gray gift. At worst, it was a black gift—a small bomb of popular design, which would blow his head off after the elapse of several anxiety-ridden days.

Marduk was not suicidal; he knew that he could not wear that damned ring. But he also knew that he *had* to wear that damned ring. Thus, he found himself facing a classic Celsian dilemma.

"Would they do that to *me?*" Marduk asked himself. "Just because I rezoned their dirty old residential neighborhood for heavy industry, and entered into an agreement with the Landlord's Guild to raise their rents 320 percent in return for a promise of new plumbing within fifty years? I mean to say, good Lord, I've never pretended to be *omniscient*; I may have made mistakes here and there, I freely admit it. But is that sufficient cause to commit what anyone must view as a deeply antisocial act?"

The ring ticked merrily away, tickling his snout and alarming his senses. Marduk thought of other officials whose heads had been blown off by dimwitted hotheads. Yes, it might very possibly be a black gift.

"Those stupid molters!" Marduk snarled, relieving his feelings with an insult he would never have dared voice in public. He was feeling sorely aggrieved. You worked your hearts out for those slack-skinned, wart-nosed idiots, and what was your reward? A bomb to wear in your nose!

For one hectic moment he contemplated throwing the ring into the nearest chlorine tank. *That* would show them! And there was precedent for it. Had not the saintly Voreeg spurned the Total Offering of the Three Ghosts?

Yes ... but the Ghosts' Offering, according to accepted exegesis, had been a subtle attack upon the spirit of Gift-Giving, and therefore at the very core of society; for by making a Total Offering, they had precluded the possibility of any future gifts.

Besides—what was admirable for a Saint of the Second Kingdom would be execrable for a petty official of the Tenth Democracy. Saints can do anything; ordinary men must do what is expected of them.

Marduk's shoulders slumped. He plastered warm mud on his feet, but it brought no relief. There was no way out. One Celsian could not stand alone against organized society. He would have to wear the ring, and wait for the mind-splitting moment when the tick stopped. . . .

But wait! There was a way! Yes, yes, he could see it now! It would take clever arrangement; but if he brought it off, he could have safety *and* social approval. If only that damned ring gave him time. . . .

Marduk Kras made several urgent calls, and arranged for himself to be ordered to the planet Taami II (the Tahiti of the Ten-Star Region on urgent business. Not corporeally, of course; no responsible official would spend local funds to ship his body across a hundred light years when all that was required was his mind. Frugal, trustworthy Marduk would travel by Mindswap. He would satisfy the form, if not the spirit, of Celsian custom by leaving his body behind with the gift ring ticking merrily in its nose.

He had to find a mind to inhabit his body during his absence. But that was not difficult. There are too many minds in the galaxy, and not enough bodies to go around. (Why this should be, no one really knows. After all, everyone was given one of each to begin with. But some people always seem to end up with more than they need, be it wealth, power, or bodies; and some with less.)

Marduk got in touch with Hermit Enterprises (Bodies for Any Purpose). The hermit had just the thing for him: a clean-cut young Terran male who was in imminent danger of losing his life, and was willing to take his chances with a ticking nose ring.

Thus Marvin Flynn came to Celsus V.

For once there was no need to hurry. Upon arrival, Marvin was able to follow prescribed Swapping procedure. He lay perfectly still, growing slowly accustomed to his new corpus. He tested his limbs, checked out his senses, and scanned the primary culture-configuration load as radiated from the forebrain for analogue and similitude factors. Then he sized up the hindbrain emotional end structure factor for crux, nadir and saddlepoint. Nearly all of this was automatic.

He found the Celsian body a good fit, with a high aspect of jointure and an excellent main-sequence random-dispersion pattern. There were problems, of course: the delta curve was absurdly elliptic, and the UYP's (universal Y points) were falciform rather than trapezoidal. But you had to expect that on a Type 3B planet; under normal circumstances, it would never cause him any trouble.

Taken all in all, it was a body-environment-culture-role cluster with which he could empathize and identify.

"Feels pretty good," Marvin summed up for himself. "If only that damned nose ring doesn't blow up."

He got up and took stock of his surroundings. The first thing he saw was a note that Marduk Kras had left for him, tied to his wrist to he wouldn't overlook it.

Dear Swapper, [it read]

Welcome to Celsus! I realize that you may not feel very welcome, under the circumstances, and I regret it nearly as much as you do. But I would advise you sincerely to put all thought of sudden demise out of your mind, and concentrate instead on having a pleasant vacation. It may console you to know that the statistical incidence of death by black gift is no greater than that of being killed in a plutonium-mine accident, if you happened to be a plutonium miner. So relax and enjoy yourself.

My apartment and all that is in it are yours to enjoy. My body also, though I trust you will not overstrain it or keep it out too late or feed it an excess of intoxicating beverages. It has a weak left wrist, so be careful if you should have to lift any heavy weights. Good luck, and try not to worry, since anxiety never yet solved a problem.

P.S. I know you are a gentleman and would not try to remove the nose ring. But I thought I should tell you that you can't anyhow because it is locked in place with a microscopic Jayverg Bonded Molecular Padlock. Goodbye again, and do try to put all this unpleasantness out of mind and enjoy your two weeks on our lovely planet.

Your Sincere Friend,
Marduk Kras

At first Marvin was irritated by the note. But then he laughed and crumpled it up. Marduk was undoubtedly a scoundrel, but he was a likable one, and not ungenerous. Marvin decided to make the best of his dubious bargain, forget about the putative bomb nestling just above his lip, and enjoy his time on Celsus.

He went on an exploration of his new home, and was well satisfied with what he found. It was a bachelor burrow, designed for residence rather than for reproduction. Its main construction feature—pentabrachation—reflected Kras's status as a public official. Less fortunate sorts had to get by with three or four gallery systems; and in the slums of North Bogger, whole families were crowded into wretched mono- and duo-brachate systems. Housing reform had been promised in the near future, however.

The kitchen was neat and modern, and well stocked with gourmet items. There were jars of candied annelids, and a bowl of exotic Alcyonium Salad mixture, and delicious tidbits of Tubipora, Pennatula, Gorgonia, and Renilla. There was a can of Goose Barnacle in rotifer and orchid sauce, and a quick-frozen package of sweet and sour Uca. But—how like a bachelor—there were no staples, not even a gastropod loaf or a bottle of carbonated Ginger Honey.

98

Wandering down the long, curving galleries, Marvin found the music room. Marduk had not stinted here. A gigantic Imperial amplifier dominated the room, flanked by two Tyrant-model speakers. Marduk used a Whirlpool semi-mix microphone, with a forty bbc. channel rejection, an "expanding" type sense-discrimination selector, with a floating throat-slot "passive" director. Pickup was by image regeneration, but there was provision for changing over to decay modulation. Although not professional in quality, it was a very good amateur rig.

The heart of the system, of course, was the Insectarium. This particular one was an Ingenuator, the Super-Max model, with both automatic and manual selection and mixture controls, regulated feed and disposal, and various maximizing and minimizing features.

Marvin selected a grasshopper gavotte (Korestal, 431B) and listened to the thrilling tracheal obbligato and the subtle bass accompaniment of the paired Malphigian tubules. Although Marvin's appreciation was casual, he was well aware of the virtuoso ability of this particular performer: a Blue-Striped Grasshopper, his second thoracic segment pulsating slightly, visible in his own compartment of the Insectarium.

Leaning down, Marvin nodded in appreciation. The Blue-Striped Grasshopper clicked mandibles, then turned back to his music. (He had been bred especially for treble and brilliance, a flashy performer, more showy than sound. But Marvin did not know this.)

Marvin turned off the selection, flipped the status switch from Active to Dormant mode; the grasshopper went back to sleep. The Insectarium was well stocked, especially with Mayfly symphonies and the strange new cutworm songs, but Marvin had too much to explore to bother with music just now.

In the living room, Marvin lowered himself into a stately old clay bank (a genuine Wormstetter), rested his head against the well-worn granite headrest, and tried to relax. But the ring in his snout ticked away, a continual intrusion to his sense of well-being. He reached down and picked at random a quick-stick from a pile on a low table. He ran his antennae over the grooves, but it was no use. He couldn't concentrate on light fiction. Impatiently he threw the quick-stick aside and tried to make some plans.

But he was in the grip of an implacable dynamism. He had to assume that the moments of his life were severely limited, and those moments were passing away. He wanted to do something to commemorate his final hours. But what was there he could do?

He slid out of the Wormstetter and paced the main gallery, his claws clicking irritably. Then, coming to an abrupt decision, he went to the wardrobe room. Here he selected a new casing of gold-bronze chitin, and arranged it carefully over his shoulders. He plastered his facial bristles with perfumed glue, and arranged them *en brosse* over his cheeks. He applied a mild stiffener to his antennae, pointed them at a jaunty sixty degrees, and allowed them to droop in their attractive natural curve. Lastly, he dusted his midsection with Lavender Sand, and outlined his shoulder joints with lampblack.

Surveying himself in the mirror, he decided that the effect was not unpleasing. He was well dressed, but not dandified. Judging as objectively as he could, he decided that he was a presentable, rather scholarly-looking young

100

fellow. Not a Squig Star by any means, but definitely not a drunfiler.

He left his burrow by the main entrance, and replaced the entrance plug.

It was dusk. Stars glittered overhead; they seemed no more numerous than the myriad lights in the entrances of the countless burrows, both commercial and private, which made up the pulsating heart of the city. The sight thrilled Marvin. Surely, surely, somewhere in the endless intertwining corridors of the great city, there would be that for him which would bring pleasure. Or, at least, a soft and forgetful surcease.

Thus, Marvin walked dolorously, yet with a tremulous hopefulness, toward the hectic and beckoning Main Groove of the City, there to find what chance held out for him or fate decreed.

CHAPTER 16

WITH A LONG ROLLING STRIDE AND A CREAK-
ing of leather boots, Marvin Flynn strode down the
wooden sidewalk. Faintly there came to him the mingled
odors of sagebrush and chaparral. On either side of him
the adobe walls of the town glittered under the moon like
dull Mexican silver. From a nearby saloon there came the
strident tones of a banjo—

Frowning deeply, Marvin stopped in midstride. Sagebrush? Saloons? What was going on around here?

"Something wrong, stranger?" a harsh voice intoned.

Flynn whirled. A figure stepped out of the shadows
near the General Store. It was a saddlebum, a snuffling,
slump-shouldered loafer with a dusty black hat crushed
comically on his begrimed forehead.

"Yes, something is very wrong," Marvin said. "Everything seems—strange."

" 'Tain't nothing to be alarmed about," the saddlebum
reassured him. "You have merely changed your system of

metaphoric reference, and the Lord knows there's no crime in that. As a matter of fact, you should be happy to give up those dreary animal-insect comparisons."

"There was nothing wrong with my comparisons," Marvin said. "After all, I am on Celsus V, and I *do* live in a burrow."

"So what?" the saddlebum said. "Haven't you any imagination?"

"I've got plenty of imagination!" Marvin said indignantly. "But that's hardly the point. I simply mean that it is inconsistent to think like a cowboy on Earth when one is actually a sort of molelike creature on Celsus."

"It can't be helped," the saddlebum said. "What's happened is, you've overloaded your analogizing faculty, thereby blowing a fuse. Accordingly, your perceptions have taken up the task of experimental normalization. This state is known as 'metaphoric deformation.' "

Now Marvin remembered the warning he had received from Mr. Blanders concerning this phenomenon. Metaphoric deformation, that disease of the interstellar traveler, had struck him suddenly and without warning.

He knew that he should be alarmed, but instead felt only a mild surprise. His emotions were consistent with his perceptions, since a change unperceived is a change unfelt.

"When," Marvin asked, "will I start to see things as they really are?"

"That last is a question for a philosopher," the saddlebum told him. "But speaking in a limited fashion, this particular syndrome will pass if you ever get back to Earth. But if you continue traveling the process of perceptual analogizing will increase; though occasional

104

short-lived remissions into your primary situation-perception context may be expected."

Marvin found that interesting, but unalarming. He hitched up his jeans and said, "Waal, reckon a man's gotta play out the hand that's dealt to him, and I ain't about to stand here all night jawing about it. Just who are you, stranger?"

"I," said the saddlebum, with a certain smugness, "am he without whom your dialogue would be impossible. I am Necessity personified; without me, you would have had to remember the Theory of Metaphoric Deformation all by yourself, and I doubt that you are capable of it. You may cross my palm with silver."

"That's for gypsies," Marvin said scornfully.

"Sorry," the saddlebum said, without the least show of embarrassment. "Got a tailor-made?"

"Got the makings," Marvin said, flipping him a sack of Bull Durham. He contemplated his new companion for a moment, then said, "Waal, yore a mangy-looking critter, and it seems to me yore half jackass and half prairie dog. But I reckon I'm stuck with you no matter who you are."

"Bravo," the saddlebum said gravely. "You conquer change of context with that same sureness with which an ape conquers a banana."

"Reckon that's a tech highfalutin," Marvin said equably. "What's the next move, perfesser?"

"We shall proceed," the saddlebum said, "to yonder saloon of evil repute."

"Yippee," Marvin said, and strode lean-hipped through the batwinged saloon doors.

Within the saloon, a female attached herself to Marvin's arm. She looked up at him with a smile of vermilion bas-relief. Her unfocused eyes were penciled in imitation of gaiety; her flaccid face was painted with the lying hieroglyphics of animation.

"C'mon upstairs with me, kid," the grisly beldame cried. "Lotsa fun, lotsa laughs!"

"It is droll to realize," the saddlebum said, "that Custom has decreed this lady's mask, proclaiming that those who sell pleasure must portray enjoyment. It is a hard demand, my friends, and not imposed upon any other occupation. For note: the fishwife is allowed to hate herring, the vegetable man may be allergic to turnips, and even the newspaper boy is permitted his illiteracy. Not even the blessed saints are required to enjoy their holy martyrdoms. Only the humble sellers of pleasure are required, like Tantalus, to be forever expectant of an untouchable feast."

"Yer friend's a great little kidder, ain't he?" the termagant said. "But I like you best, baby, 'cause you make me go all mush inside."

From the virago's neck there hung a pendant upon which was strung in miniature a skull, a piano, an arrow, a baby's shoe, and a yellowed tooth.

"What are those?" Marvin asked.

"Symbols," she said.

"Of what?"

"Come on upstairs, and I'll show you, sweety-ass."

"And thus," the saddlebum intoned, "we perceive the true unmediated confrontation of the aroused feminine nature, 'gainst which our masculine fancies seem mere baby's toys."

"C'mon!" the harpy cried, wriggling her gross body in

106

a counterfeit of passion all the more frightening because it was real. "Upstairs to bed!" she shouted, pressing against Marvin with a breast the size and consistency of an empty Mongolian saddlebag. "I'll really show ya somepin!" she cried, entwining his thews with a heavy white leg, somewhat grimy and heavily varicosed. "When ya git loved by *me*," she howled, "you'll damned well know you been loved!" And she ground lasciviously against him with her pudenda, which was as heavily armored as the forehead of a Tyrannosaurus.

"Well, er, thank you so terribly much anyhow," Marvin said, "but I don't think just at the moment I—"

"You don't want no *lovin'*?" the woman asked incredulously.

"Well, actually, I can't really say that I do."

The woman planted knobkerry fists on tom-tom hips and said, "That I should live to see this day!" But then she softened, and said, "Turn not away from Venus' sweet-perfumed home of pleasure! Thou must strive, sir, to overcome this most unseemly gesture of unmanliness. Come, my lord! The bugle sounds; it awaits thee now to mount and fiercely press thy charge!"

"Oh, I rather think not," Marvin said, laughing hollowly.

She seized him by the throat with a hand the size and shape of a Chilean poncho. "You'll do it *now*, you lousy cowardly inward-directed goddamn narcissist bastard, and you'll do it good and proper, or by Ares I'll snap your scrawny windpipe like a Michaelmas chicken!"

A tragedy seemed in the making, for the woman's passion rendered her incapable of a judicious modification of her demands, while Marvin's reputed great vaulting lance had shrunken to the size of a pea. (Thus blind nature, by defending him from one assault, tendered provocation for another.)

Luckily the saddlebum, following the dictates of his wit if not his predilection, snatched a fan out of his gun belt, leaned forward simpering, and tapped the enraged woman on her rhinocerine upper arm.

"Don't you dare hurt him!" the saddlebum said, his voice a squeaky contralto.

Marvin, quick if not apt, rejoindered, "Yes, tell her to stop *pawing* me! I mean to say it is simply too much, one cannot even stroll out of one's house in the evening without encountering some *disgraceful* incident—"

"Don't cry, for God's sake, don't cry!" the saddlebum said. "You know I can't stand it when you cry!"

"I am *not* crying!" Marvin said, snuffling. "It is just that she has ruined this shirt. Your present!"

"I'll get you another!" the saddlebum said. "But I cannot abide another scene!"

The woman was staring at them slack-jawed, and Marvin was able to utilize her moment of inattention by taking a pry bar out of his tool kit, setting it under her swollen red fingers, and prying himself free of her grip. Seizing the dwindling moment of opportunity, Marvin and the saddlebum sprinted out the door, leaped around the corner, broad-jumped across the street, and polevaulted to freedom.

CHAPTER 17

ONCE CLEAR OF THE IMMEDIATE DANGER,
Marvin came abruptly to his senses. The scales of
metaphoric deformation fell away for the moment, and
he experienced a perceptual experiential remission. It
was all too painfully apparent now that the "saddlebum"
was actually a large parasite beetle of the species *S.
Cthulu.* There could be no mistake about this, since the
Cthulu beetle is characterized by a secondary salivary
duct located just below and slightly to the left of the
subesophegal ganglion.

These beetles feed upon borrowed emotions, their own
having long ago atrophied. Typically, they lurk in dark
and shadowy places, waiting for a careless Celsian to
pass within range of their segmented maxilla. That is
what happened to Marvin.

Realizing this, Marvin directed at the bettle an emotion of anger so powerful that the Cthulu, victim of its
own hyperacute emotional receptors, fell over uncon-

scious in the road. That done, Marvin readjusted his gold-bronze casing, stiffened his antennae, and continued down the road.

He came to a bridge that crossed a great flowing river of sand. Standing on the center span, he gazed downward into the black depths that rolled inexorably onward to the mysterious sand sea. Half-hypnotized he gazed, the nose ring beating its quick tattoo of mortality three times faster than the beat of his hearts. And he thought:

Bridges are receptacles of opposed ideas. Their horizontal distance speaks to us of our transcendence; their vertical declivity reminds us unalterably of the imminence of failure, the sureness of death. We push outward across obstacles, but the primordial fall is forever beneath our feet. We build, construct, fabricate; but death is the supreme architect, who shapes heights only that there may be depths.

O Celsians, throw your well-wrought bridges across a thousand rivers, and tie together the disparate contours of the planet; your mastery is for naught, for the land is still beneath you, still waiting, still patient. Celsians, you have a road to follow, but it leads assuredly to death. Celsians, despite your cunning, you have one lesson still to learn: the heart is fashioned to receive the spear, and all other effects are extraneous.

These were Marvin's thoughts as he stood on the bridge. And a great longing overcame him, a desire to be finished with desire, to forego pleasure and pain, to quit the petty modes of achievement and failure, to have done with distractions, and get on with the business of life, which was death.

Slowly he climbed to the rail, and there stood poised

110

over the twisting currents of sand. Then, out of the corner of his eye, he saw a shadow detach itself from a pillar, move tentatively to the rail, stand erect, poise itself over the abyss and lean precariously outward—

"Stop! Wait!" Marvin cried. His own desire for destruction had been abruptly terminated. He saw only a fellow creature in peril.

The shadowy figure gasped, and abruptly lunged toward the yawning river below. Marvin moved simultaneously and managed to catch an ankle.

The ensuing wrench almost pulled him over the rail. But recovering quickly, Marvin attached suckers to the porous stone sidewalk, spread his lower limbs for maximum purchase, wrapped two upper limbs around a light pole, and maintained a tenacious grip with his remaining two arms.

There was a moment of charged equilibrium; then Marvin's strength prevailed over the weight of the would-be suicide. Slowly, carefully, Marvin pulled, shifting his grip from tarsus to tibia, hauling without respite until he had brought that person to a point of safety on the roadbed of the bridge.

All recollection of his own self-destructive desires had left him. He strode forward and grasped the suicider by the shoulders, shaking fiercely.

"You damned fool!" Marvin shouted. "What kind of a coward are you? Only an idiot or a madman takes an out like that. Haven't you any guts at all, you damned—"

He stopped in midexpletive. The would-be suicide was facing him, trembling, eyes averted. And now Marvin perceived, for the first time, that he had rescued a woman.

CHAPTER 18

LATER, IN A PRIVATE BOOTH IN A BRIDGE-
side restaurant, Marvin apologized for his harsh words,
which had been torn from him by shock rather than conviction. But the woman, gracefully clicking her claw, refused to accept his apology.

"Because you are right," she said. "My attempt was the
act of an idiot or a madwoman, or both. Your analysis
was correct, I fear. You should have let me jump."

Marvin perceived how fair she was. A small woman,
coming barely to his upper thorax, she was exquisitely
made. Her midbody had the true sweet cylinder curves,
and her proud head sat slightly forward of her body at a
heart-wrenching five degrees from the vertical. Her features were perfection, from the nicely bulged forehead to
the angular sweep of jaw. Her twin ovipositors were
modestly hidden behind a white satin sash, cut in prin-
cess style and revealing just a tantalizing suggestion of

113

the shining green flesh beneath them. Her legs, all of them, were clad in orange windings, draped to reveal the lissome segmentation of the joints.

A would-be suicide she may have been; but she was also the most stunning beauty that Marvin had seen on Celsus. His throat went dry at the sight of her, and his pulse began to race. He found that he was staring at the white satin that concealed and revealed her high-tilted ovipositors. He turned away, and found that he was looking at the sensual marvel of a long, segmented limb. Blushing furiously, he forced himself to look at the puckered beauty-scar on her forehead.

She seemed unconscious of his fervent attention. Unself-consciously she said, "Perhaps we should introduce ourselves—under the circumstances!"

They both laughed immoderately at her witticism. "My name is Marvin Flynn," Marvin said.

"Mine is Phthistia Held," the young woman said.

"I'll call you Cathy, if you don't mind," Marvin said.

They both laughed again. Then Cathy grew serious. Taking note of the too-quick passage of time, she said, "I must thank you again. And now I must leave."

"Of course," Marvin said, rising. "When may I see you again?"

"Never," she said in a low voice.

"But I must!" Marvin said. "I mean to say, now that I've found you I can never let you go."

She shook her head sadly. "Once in a while," she murmured, "will you give one little thought to me?"

"We must not say goodbye!" Marvin said.

"Oh, you'll get by," she replied, not cruelly.

"I'll never smile again," Marvin told her.

114

"Somebody else will be taking my place," she predicted.

"You are temptation!" he shouted in a fury.

"We are like two ships that pass in the night," she corrected.

"Will we never meet again?" Marvin queried.

"Time alone can tell."

"My prayer is to be there with you," Marvin said hopefully.

"East of the Sun and West of the Moon," she intoned.

"You're mean to me," Marvin pouted.

"I didn't know what time it was," she said. "But I know what time it is now!" And so saying, she whirled and darted out the door.

Marvin watched her leave, then sat down at the bar. "One for my baby, and one for the road," he told the bartender.

"A woman's a two-face," the bartender commented sympathetically, pouring a drink.

"I got the mad-about-her-sad-without-her blues," Marvin replied.

"A fellow needs a girl," the bartender told him.

Marvin finished his drink and held out his glass. "A pink cocktail for a blue lady," he ordered.

"She may be weary," the bartender suggested.

"I don't know why I love her like I do," Marvin stated. "But at least I do know why there's no sun up in the sky. In my solitude she haunts me like a tinkling piano in the next apartment. But I'll be around no matter how she treats me now. Maybe it was just one of those things; yet I'll remember April and her, and the evening breeze caressed the trees but not for me, and—"

115

There is no telling how long Marvin might have continued his lament had not a voice at the level of his ribs and two feet to his left whispered, "Hey, Meester."

Marvin turned and saw a small, plump, raggedly dressed Celsian sitting on the next bar stool.

"What is it?" Marvin asked brusquely.

"You maybe want see thees muchacha so beautiful other time?"

"Yes, I do. But what can you—"

"I am private investigator tracer of lost persons satisfaction guaranteed or not one cent in tribute."

"What kind of an accent have you got?" Marvin asked.

"Lambrobian," the investigator said. "My name is Juan Valdez and I come from the fiesta lands below the border to make my fortune here in big city of the Norte."

"Sandback," the bartender snarled.

"What thees theeng you call me?" the little Lombrobian said, with suspicious mildness.

"I called you a sandback, you lousy little sandback," the bartender snarled.

"That ees what I thought," said Valdez. He reached into his cummerbund, took out a long, double-edged knife, and drove it into the bartender's heart, killing him instantly.

"I am a mild man, señor," he said to Marvin. "I am not a man quickly to take offense. Indeed, in my home village of Montana Verde de los Tres Picos, I am considered a harmless man. I ask nothing more than to be allowed to cultivate my peyote buds in the high mountains of Lombrobia under the shade of that tree which we call 'the sun hat,' for these are the bes' peyote buds in all the world."

116

"I can understand that," Marvin said.

"Yet still," Valdez said, more sternly, "when an exploitator del norte insults me, and by implication, defames those who gave me birth and nurtured me—why then, señor, a blinding red mist descends over my field of vision and my knife springs to my hand unaided, and proceeds from there nonstop to the heart of the betrayer of the children of the poor."

"It could happen to anyone," Marvin said.

"And yet," Valdez said, "despite my keen sense of honor, I am essentially childlike, intuitive, and easygoing."

"I had noticed that, as a matter of fact," Marvin said.

"But yet. Enough of that. Now, you wish hire me investigation find girl? But of course. El buen pano en el arca se vende, verdad?"

"Si, hombre," Marvin replied, laughing. "Y el deseo vence al miedo!"

"Pues, adelante!" And arm in arm the two comrades marched out into the night of a thousand brilliant stars like the lance points of a mighty host.

CHAPTER 19

ONCE OUTSIDE THE RESTAURANT, VALDEZ turned his moustached brown face to the heavens and located the constellation Invidius, which, in northern latitudes, points unerringly to the north-northeast. With this as a base line, he established cross references, using the wind on his cheek (blowing west at five miles per hour), and the moss on the trees (growing on the northerly sides of decidupis trunks at one millimeter per diem). He allowed for a westerly error of one foot per mile (drift), and a southerly error of five inches per hundred yards (combined tropism effects). Then, with all factors accounted for, he began walking in a south-southwesterly direction.

Marvin followed. Within an hour they had left the city, and were proceeding through a stubbled farming district. Another hour put them beyond the last signs of civilization, in a wilderness of tumbled granite and greasy feldspar.

Valdez showed no signs of stopping, and Marvin began to feel vague stirrings of doubt.

"Just where, exactly, are we going?" he asked at last.

"To find your Cathy," Valdez replied, his teeth flashing white in his good-humored burnt-sienna face.

"Does she really live this far from the city?"

"I have no idea where she lives," Valdez replied, shrugging.

"You don't?"

"No, I don't."

Marvin stopped abruptly. "But you said that you did know!"

"I never said or implied that," Valdez said, his umber forehead wrinkling. "I said that I would help you find her."

"But if you don't know where she lives—"

"It is quite unimportant," Valdez said, holding up a stern musteline forefinger. "Our quest has nothing to do with finding where Cathy *lives;* our quest, pure and simple, is to find *Cathy.* That, at least, was my understanding."

"Yes, of course," Marvin said. "But if we're not going to where she lives, then where are we going?"

"To where she weel be," Valdez replied serenely.

"Oh," Marvin said.

They walked on through towering mineral marvels, coming at last into scrubby foothills that lay like tired walruses around the gleaming blue whale of a lofty mountain range. Another hour passed, and Marvin again grew disquieted. But this time he expressed his anxiety in a roundabout fashion, hoping by guile to gain insight.

"Have you known Cathy long?" he asked.

120

"I have never had the good fortune to meet her," Valdez replied.

"Then you saw her for the first time in the restaurant with me?"

"Unfortunately I did not even see her there, since I was in the men's room passing a kidney stone during the time of your conversation with her. I may have caught a glimpse of her as she turned from you and departed; but more likely I saw only the Doppler effect produced by the swinging red door."

"Then you know nothing whatsoever about Cathy?"

"Only the little I have heard from you, which, frankly, amounts to practically nothing."

"Then how," Marvin asked, "can you possibly take me to where she will be?"

"It is simple enough," Valdez said. "A moment's reflection should clear the matter for you."

Marvin reflected for several moments, but the matter stayed refractory.

"Consider it logically," Valdez said. "What is my problem? *To find Cathy*. What do I know about Cathy? Nothing."

"That doesn't sound so good," Marvin said.

"But it is only half of the problem. Granted that I know nothing about Cathy, what do I know about *Finding*?"

"What?" Marvin asked.

"It happens that I know everything about Finding," Valdez said triumphantly, gesturing with his graceful terra-cotta hands. "For it happens that I am an expert in the Theory of Searches!"

"The what?" Marvin asked.

"The Theory of Searches!" Valdez said, a little less triumphantly.

"I see," Marvin said, unimpressed. "Well . . . that's great, and I'm sure it's a very good theory. But if you don't know anything about Cathy, I don't see how any theory will help."

Valdez sighed, not unpleasantly, and touched his moustache with a puce-colored hand. "My friend, if you knew all about Cathy—her habits, friends, desires, dislikes, hopes, fears, dreams, intentions, and the like—do you think you would be able to find her?"

"I'm sure I could," Marvin said.

"Even without knowing the Theory of Searches?"

"Yes."

"Well then," Valdez said, "apply that same reasoning to the reverse condition. I know all there is to know about the Theory of Searches, and therefore I need to know nothing about Cathy."

"Are you sure it's the same thing?" Marvin asked.

"It has to be. After all, an equation is an equation. Solving from one end may take longer than from the other end, but cannot affect the outcome. In fact, we are really quite fortunate to know nothing about Cathy. Specific data sometimes has a way of interfering with the well-wrought operation of a theory. But we shall suffer no such discomfiture in this instance."

They marched steadily upward, across the steepening face of a mountain slope. A bitter wind screamed and buffeted at them, and patches of hoar-frost began to appear underfoot. Valdez talked about his researches into the Theory of Searches, citing the following typical cases: Hector looking for Lysander, Adam questing after

122

Eve, Galahad reconnoitering for the Holy Grail, Fred C. Dobbs's seeking the Treasure of the Sierra Madre, Edwin Arlington Robinson's perquisitions for colloquial self-expression in a typically American milieu, Gordon Sly's investigations of Naiad McCarthy, energy's pursuit of entropy, God's hunt for man, and yang's pursual of yin.

"From these specifics," Valdez said, "we derive the general notion of Search and its most important corollaries."

Marvin was too miserable to answer. It had suddenly occurred to him that one could die in this chill and waterless wasteland.

"Amusingly enough," Valdez said, "the Theory of Searches forces upon us the immediate conclusion that nothing can be truly (or ideally) lost. Consider: for a thing to be *lost*, it would require *a place to be lost in*. But no such place can be found, since simple multiplicity carries no implication of qualitative differentiation. In Search terms, every place is like every other place. Therefore, we replace the concept *Lost* with the concept of *indeterminate placement*, which, of course, is susceptible to logico-mathematical analysis."

"But if Cathy isn't really lost," Marvin said, "then we can't really find her."

"That statement is true, as far as it goes," Valdez said. "But of course, it is merely Ideal notion, and of little value in this instance. For operational purposes we must modify the Theory of Searches. In fact, we must reverse the major premise of the theory and reaccept the original concepts of Lost and Found."

"It sounds very complicated," Marvin said.

"The complication is more apparent than real," Valdez

reassured him. "An analysis of the problem yields the result. We take the proposition: 'Marvin searches for Cathy.' That seems fairly to describe our situation, does it not?"

"I think it does," Marvin said cautiously.

"Well then, what does the statement imply?"

"It implies—it implies that I search for Cathy."

Valdez shook his nut-brown head in annoyance. "Look deeper, my impatient young friend! Identity is not inference! The statement expresses the activity of your quest, and therefore implies the passivity of Cathy's state-of-being-lost. But this cannot be true. Her passivity is unacceptable, since ultimately one searches for oneself, and no one is exempt from that search. We must accept Cathy's search for you (herself), just as we accept your search for her (yourself). Thus we achieve our primary permutation: 'Marvin searches for Cathy who searches for Marvin.' "

"Do you really think she's looking for me?" Marvin asked.

"Of course she is, whether she knows it or not. After all, she is a person in her own right; she cannot be considered an Object, a mere something-lost. We must grant her autonomy, and realize that if you find her, then, equally, she finds you."

"I never thought of that," Marvin said.

"Well, it's simple enough once you understand the theory," Valdez said. "Now, to ensure our success, we must decide upon the optimum form of Search. Obviously, if both of you are actively questing, your chances of finding each other are considerably lessened. Consider two people seeking one another up and down the endless crowded aisles of a great department store, and contrast

124

that with the improved strategy of one seeking, and the other standing at a fixed position and waiting to be found. The mathematics are a little intricate, so you will just have to take my word for it. The best chance of you/ her finding her/you will be for one to search, and the other to allow himself/herself to be searched for. Our deepest folk wisdom has always known this, of course."

"So what do we do?"

"I have just told you!" Valdez cried. "One must search, the other must wait. Since we have no control over Cathy's actions, we assume that she is following her instincts and looking for you. Therefore you must fight down your instincts and wait, thereby allowing her to find you."

"All I do is wait?"

"That's right."

"And you really think she'll find me?"

"I would stake my life on it."

"Well . . . all right. But in that case, where are we going now?"

"To a place where you will wait. Technically, it is called a Location-Point."

Marvin looked confused, so Valdez explained further. "Mathematically, all places are of equal potentiality insofar as the chances of her finding you are concerned. Therefore we are able to choose an arbitrary Location-Point."

"What Location-Point have you chosen?" Marvin asked.

"Since it made no real difference," Valdez said, "I selected the village of Montana Verde de los Tres Picos, in Adelante Province, in the country of Lombrobia."

"That's your home town, isn't it?" Marvin asked.

"As a matter of fact, it is," Valdez said, mildly surprised and amused. "That, I suppose, is why it came so quickly to my mind."

"Isn't Lombrobia a long way off?"

"A considerable distance," Valdez admitted. "But our time will not be wasted, since I will teach you logic, and also the folksongs of my country."

"It isn't fair," Marvin muttered.

"My friend," Valdez told him, "when you accept help, you must be prepared to take what one is capable of giving, not what you would like to receive. I have never denied my human limitations; but it is ungrateful of you to refer to them."

Marvin had to be content with that, since he didn't think he could find his way back to the city unaided. So they marched on through the mountains, and they sang many folksongs, but it was too cold for logic.

CHAPTER 20

ONWARD THEY MARCHED, UP THE POLISHED mirror face of a vast mountain. The wind whistled and screamed, tore at their clothing and tugged at their straining fingers. Treacherous honeycomb ice crumbled under their feet as they struggled for footholds, their buffeted bodies plastered to the icy mountain wall and moving leechlike up its dazzling surface.

Valdez bore up through it all with a saintlike equanimity. "Eet ees deefecult," he grinned. "And yet—for the love which you bear for thees woman—eet ees all worthwhile, sí?"

"Yeah, sure," Marvin mumbled. "I guess it is." But in truth, he was beginning to doubt it. After all, he had known Cathy only for less than an hour.

An avalanche thundered past them, and tons of white death screamed past—inches from their strained and clinging bodies. Valdez smiled with serenity. Flynn frowned with anxiety.

"Beyond all obstacles," Valdez intoned, "lies that summit of accomplishment which is the face and form of the beloved."

"Yeah, sure," Marvin said.

Spears of ice, shaken loose from a high dokalma, whirled and flashed around them. Marvin thought about Cathy and found that he was unable to remember what she looked like. It struck him that love at first sight was overrated.

A high precipice loomed before them. Marvin looked at it, and at the shimmering ice fields beyond, and came to the conclusion that the game was really not worth the candle.

"I think," Marvin said, "that we should turn back."

Valdez smiled subtly, pausing on the very edge of the vertiginous descent into that wintry hell of suicidally shaped snow slides.

"My frien'," he said, "I know why you say this."

"You do?" Marvin asked.

"Of course. It is obvious that you do not wish me to risk my life on the continuance of your insensate and magnificent quest. And it is equally obvious that you intend to plunge on, alone."

"It is?" Marvin asked.

"Certainly. It would be apparent to the most casual observer that you are driven to seek your love through any and all dangers, by virtue of the unyielding nature of your personality. And it is equally clear that your generous and high-spirited mentality would be disturbed at the idea of involving one whom you consider a close friend and bosom companion in so perilous a venture."

"Well," Marvin began, "I'm not sure—"

128

"But I am sure," Valdez said. "And I reply to your unspoken question as follows: Friendship bears this similarity to love: it transcends all limits."

"Huh," Marvin said.

"Therefore," Valdez said, "I shall not abandon you. We shall go on together, into the maw of death, if need be, for the sake of your beloved Cathy."

"Well, that's very nice of you," Marvin said, eyeing the precipice ahead. "But I really didn't know Cathy very well, and I don't know how well suited we would be; so all in all, maybe it would be best if we got out of here—"

"Your words lack conviction, my young friend," Valdez laughed. "I beg of you not to worry about my safety."

"As a matter of fact," Marvin said, "I was worrying about *my* safety."

"No use!" Valdez cried gaily. "Hot passion betrays the studied coolness of your words. Forward, my friend!"

Valdez seemed determined to force him to Cathy's side whether he wanted to go or not. The only solution seemed to be a quick blow to the jaw, after which he would drag Valdez and himself back to civilization. He edged forward.

Valdez edged back. "Ah no, my friend!" he cried. "Again, overweening love has rendered your motives transparent. To knock me out, is it not? Then, after making sure I was safe and comfortable and well-provisioned, you would plunge alone into the white wilderness. But I refuse to comply. We go on together, compadre!"

And, shouldering all their provisions, Valdez began his descent of the precipice. Marvin could do nothing but follow.

We shall not bore the reader with an account of that great march across the Moorescu Mountains, nor with the agonies suffered by the love-dazzled young Flynn and his steadfast companion. Nor shall we delineate the strange hallucinations that beset the travelers, nor the temporary state of insanity that Valdez suffered when he thought he was a bird and able to fly across thousand-foot drops. Nor would any but the scholarly be interested in the psychological process by which Marvin was moved, through a contemplation of his own sacrifices, to a fondness for the young lady in question, and then to a *strong* fondness, and then to a sensation of love, and then to an overweening passion of love.

Suffice it to say that all of these things happened, and that the journey across the mountains occupied many days and brought about many emotions. And at last it came to an end.

Arriving at a last mountain crest, Marvin looked down and saw, instead of ice fields, green pastures and rolling forests under a summer sun, and a little village nestled in the crook of a gentle river.

"Is—is that—?" Marvin began.

"Yes, my son," Valdez said quietly. "That is the village of Montana de los Tres Picos, in Adelante Province, in the country of Lombrobia, in the valley of the Blue Moon."

Marvin thanked his old guru—for no other name was applicable to the role that the devious and saintly Valdez had played—and began his descent to the Location Point where his wait for Cathy would begin.

CHAPTER 21

MONTANA DE LOS TRES PICOS! HERE, SUR-
rounded by crystal lakes and high mountains, a simple, good-hearted peasantry engage in unhurried labor
beneath the swan-necked palms. At midday and mid-
night one may hear the plaintive notes of a guitar echo
down the crenellated walls of the old castle. Nut-brown
maidens tend the dusty grape vines while a moustached
cacique watches, his whip curled sleepily on his hairy wrist.

To this quaint memento of a bygone age came Flynn,
led by the faithful Valdez.

Just outside the village, on a gentle rise of land, there
was an inn, or posada. To this place Valdez directed
them.

"But is this really the best place to wait?" Marvin
asked.

"No, it is not," Valdez said, with a knowing smile. "But
by choosing it instead of the dusty town square, we avoid

131

the fallacy of the 'optimum.' Also, it is more comfortable here."

Marvin bowed to the moustached man's superior wisdom and made himself at home in the posada. He settled himself at an outdoor table that commanded a good view of the courtyard and of the road beyond it. He fortified himself with a flagon of wine, and proceeded to fulfill his theoretical function as called for by the Theory of Searches: viz., he waited.

Within the hour, Marvin beheld a tiny dark figure moving slowly along the gleaming white expanse of the road. Closer it came, the figure of a man no longer young, his back bent beneath the weight of a heavy cylindrical object. At last the man raised his haggard head and stared directly into Marvin's eyes.

"Uncle Max!" Marvin cried.

"Why, hello, Marvin," Uncle Max replied. "Would you mind pouring me a glass of wine? This is a very dusty road."

Marvin poured the glass of wine, scarcely believing the testimony of his senses; for Uncle Max had unaccountably disappeared some ten years ago. He had last been seen playing golf at the Fairhaven Country Club.

"What happened to you?" Marvin asked.

"I stumbled into a time warp on the twelfth hole," Uncle Max said. "If you ever get back to Earth, Marvin, you might speak to the club manager about it. I have never been a *complainer*; but it seems to me that the greens committee ought to know about this, and possibly build a small fence or other enclosing structure. I do not

132

care so much for myself, but it might cause a nasty scandal if a child fell in."

"I'll certainly tell them," Marvin said. "But Uncle Max, where are you going now?"

"I have an appointment in Samarra," Uncle Max said. "Thank you for the wine, my boy, and take good care of yourself. By the way; did you know that your nose is ticking?"

"Yes," Marvin said. "It's a bomb."

"I suppose you know what you're doing," Max said. "Goodbye, Marvin."

And Uncle Max trudged away down the road, his golf bag swinging from his back and a number 2 iron in his hand as a walking stick. Marvin settled back to wait.

Half an hour later, Marvin spied the figure of a woman hurrying down the road. He felt a rising sensation of anticipation, but then slumped back in his chair. It was not Cathy after all. It was only his mother.

"You're a long way from home, Mom," he said quietly.

"I know, Marvin," his mother said. "But you see, I was captured by white slavers."

"Gosh, Mom! How did it happen?"

"Well, Marvin," his mother said, "I was simply taking a Christmas basket to a poor family in Cutpurse Lane, and there was a police raid, and various other things happened, and I was drugged and awoke in Buenos Aires in a luxurious room with a man standing near me and leering and asking me in broken English if I *wanted a little fun.* And when I said no, he bent down and clasped me in his arms in an embrace that was plainly designed to be lecherous."

"Gosh! What happened then?"

"Well," his mother said, "I was lucky enough to remember a little trick that Mrs. Jasperson had told me. Did you know that you can kill a man by striking him forcibly under the nose? Well, it actually does work. I didn't like to do it, Marvin, although it seemed a good idea at the time. And so I found myself in the streets of Buenos Aires and one thing led to another and here I am."

"Won't you have some wine?" Marvin asked.

"That's very thoughtful of you," his mother said, "but I really must be on my way."

"Where?"

"To Havana," his mother said. "I have a message for Garcia. Marvin, have you a cold?"

"No, I probably sound funny because of this bomb in my nose."

"Take care of yourself, Marvin," his mother said, and hurried on.

Time passed. Marvin ate his dinner on the portico, washed it down with a flagon of Sangre de Hombre, '36, and settled back in the deep shadow cast by the whitewashed palladium. The sun stretched its golden bottom toward the mountain peaks. Down the road, the figure of a man could be seen hurrying past the inn. . . .

"Father!" Marvin cried.

"Good afternoon, Marvin," his father said, startled but hiding it well. "I must say, you turn up in some unexpected places."

"I could say the same of you," Marvin said.

His father frowned, adjusted his necktie and changed

134

his briefcase to the other hand. "There is nothing strange about me being here," he told his son. "Usually your mother drives me home from the station. But today she was delayed, and so I walked. Since I was walking, I decided to take the shortcut which goes over one side of the golf course."

"I see," Marvin said.

"I will admit," his father continued, "that this shortcut seems to have become a 'long' cut, as one might express it, for I estimate that I have been walking through this countryside for the better part of an hour, if not longer."

"Dad," Marvin said, "I don't know how to tell you this, but the fact is, you are no longer on Earth."

"I find nothing humorous about a remark like that," his father stated. "Doubtless I have gone out of my way; nor is the style of architecture what I would normally expect to find in New York State. But I am quite certain that if I continue along this road for another hundred yards or so, it will lead into Annandale Avenue, which in turn will take me to the intersection of Maple Street and Spruce Lane. From there, of course, I can easily find my way home."

"I suppose you're right," Marvin said. He had never been able to win an argument from his father.

"I must be getting along," his father said. "By the way, Marvin, were you aware that you have some sort of obstruction in your nose?"

"Yes sir," Marvin said. "It's a bomb."

His father frowned deeply, pierced him with a glance, shook his head regretfully, and marched on down the road.

"I don't understand it," Marvin remarked later to Valdez. "Why are all of these people finding me? It just doesn't seem natural."

"It isn't natural," Valdez assured him. "But it *is* inevitable, which is much more important."

"Maybe it is inevitable," Marvin said. "But it is also highly improbable."

"True," Valdez agreed. "Although we prefer to call that a forced-probability; which is to say, it is an indeterminate concomitant of the Theory of Searches."

"I'm afraid I don't fully understand that," Marvin said.

"Well, it's simple enough. The Theory of Searches is a pure theory; which is to say that on paper it works every time, with no conceivable refutation. But once we take the pure and ideal and attempt to make practical applications, we encounter difficulties, the foremost of which is the phenomenon of indeterminacy. To put it in its simplest terms, what happens is this: the presence of the Theory interferes with the working of the Theory. You see, the Theory cannot take into account the effect of its own existence upon itself. Ideally, the Theory of Searches exists in a universe in which there is no Theory of Searches. But practically—which is our concern here —the Theory of Searches exists in a world in which there *is* a Theory of Searches, which has what we call a 'mirroring' or 'doubling' effect upon itself. According to some thinkers, there is a very real danger of 'infinite duplication,' in which the Theory endlessly modifies itself in terms of prior modifications of the Theory by the Theory, coming at last to a state of entropy, in which all possibilities are equally valued. This argument is known as Von Gruemann's Fallacy, in which the error of implying

136

causality to mere sequence is self-evident. Does it become more clear?"

"I think so," Marvin said. "The only thing I don't understand is, exactly what effect does the existence of the Theory have upon the Theory?"

"I thought I had explained that," Valdez said. "The primary, or 'natural' effect of a theory of searches upon a theory of searches is of course to increase the value of lambda-chi."

"Hmm," said Marvin.

"Lambda-chi is, of course, the symbolic representation of the inverse ratio of all possible searches to all possible finds. Thus, when lambda-chi is increased through indeterminacy or other factors, the possibility of search-failure is rapidly reduced to a figure near zero, while the possibility of search-success expands quickly toward one. This is known as the Set-Expansion Factor."

"Does that mean," Marvin asked, "that because of the effect of the Theory of Searches on the Theory of Searches, which results in the Set-Expansion Factor, that all searches will be successful?"

"Exactly," Valdez said. "You have expressed it beautifully, though perhaps with insufficient rigor. All possible searches will be successful during the time, or duration, of the Set-Expansion Factor."

"I understand now," Marvin said. "According to the theory, I must find Cathy."

"Yes," Valdez said. "You must find Cathy; as a matter of fact, you must find everyone. The only limitation is the Set-Expansion Factor, or S-E."

"Oh?" Marvin asked.

"Well, naturally, all searches can only be successful

137

during the time, or duration, of S-E. But the duration of S-E is a variable which can last no less than 6.3 microseconds and no more than 1,005.34543 years."

"How long will S-E last in my particular case?" Marvin asked.

"A lot of us would like to know the answer to that one," Valdez said, with a hearty chuckle.

"You mean that you don't know?"

"I mean that it has been the labor of several lifetimes simply to discover the existence of the Set-Expansion Factor. To determine an exact numerical solution for it for all possible cases would be possible, I suppose, if S-E were a mere variable. But it happens to be a *contingent* variable, which is a very different kettle of fish. You see, the calculus of contingencies is a rather new branch of mathematics, and one that no one can pretend to have mastered."

"I was afraid of that," Marvin said.

"Science is a cruel taskmaster," Valdez agreed. Then he winked cheerfully and said, "But of course, even the cruelest taskmasters can be evaded."

"Do you mean to say there is a solution?" Marvin cried.

"Not a legitimate one, unfortunately," Valdez said. "It is what we Search Theorists call a 'bootleg solution.' That is to say, it is a pragmatic application of a formula that, statistically, has had a high degree of correlation with required solutions. But as a theory, there are no rational grounds for presuming its validity."

"Still," Marvin said, "if it works, let's try it out."

"I would really rather not," Valdez said. "Irrational formulae, no matter what their apparent degree of success, are distasteful to me, containing, as they do, distressing hints that the supreme logic of mathematics might be founded ultimately upon gross absurdities."

"I insist," Marvin said. "After all, I am the one who is Searching."

"That has nothing to do with it, mathematically speaking," Valdez said. "But I suppose you would give me no peace unless I indulged you."

Valdez sighed unhappily, schlepped a piece of paper and a stub pencil out of his rebozo, and asked, "How many coins do you have in your pocket?"

Marvin looked and replied, "Eight."

Valdez wrote down the result, then asked for the date of Marvin's birth, his social-security number, his shoe size, and height in centimeters. To this he gave a numerical value. He asked Marvin to pick a number at random between 1 and 14. With this, he added several figures of his own, then scribbled and calculated for several minutes.

"Well?" Marvin asked.

"Remember, this result is merely statistically probable," Valdez said, "and has no other grounds for credence."

Marvin nodded. Valdez said, "the duration of the Set-Expansion Factor, in your particular case, is due to expire in exactly one minute and forty-eight seconds, plus or minus five minimicroseconds."

Marvin was about to protest vehemently about the unfairness of this, and to ask why Valdez hadn't made that vital calculation earlier. But then he looked down upon the road, now glowing a singular white against the rich blue of evening.

He saw a figure moving slowly toward the posada.

"Cathy!" Marvin cried. For it was she.

"Search completed with 43 seconds of the Set-Expansion Factor unelapsed," Valdez noted. "Another experimental validation of Search Theory."

But Marvin did not hear him, for he had rushed down to the road, and there clasped the long-lost beloved in his arms. And Valdez, the wily old friend and taciturn companion of the Long March, smiled tightly to himself and ordered another bottle of wine.

CHAPTER 22

AND SO THEY WERE TOGETHER AT LAST—
beautiful Cathy, star-crossed and planet-haunted, drawn
by the strange alchemy of the Location-Point; and
Marvin, young and strong, with his swallow's flash smile
in a tanned, good-humored face, Marvin, setting out with
a young man's audacity and easy confidence to conquer
the challenge of an old and intricate universe, with
Cathy at his side, younger than he in years, yet vastly
older in her woman's inherited store of intuitive wisdom;
lovely Cathy, whose fine dark eyes seemed to hold a
brooding sorrow, an elusive shadow of anticipated sadness that Marvin was unaware of except to feel a great
and almost overwhelming desire to protect and cherish
this seemingly fragile girl with her secret, that she could
not reveal, who had come at last to him, a man without a
secret that he could reveal.

Their happiness was flawed and ennobled. There was
the bomb in Marvin's nose, ticking away the inexorable

seconds of his destiny, providing a strict metronomic measure for their dance of love. But this sense of fore-doomedness caused their opposed destinies to twine closer, and it informed their relationship with grace and meaning.

He created waterfalls for her out of the morning dew, and from the colored pebbles of a meadow stream he made a necklace more beautiful than emeralds, sadder than pearls. She caught him in her net of silken hair, she carried him down, down, into deep and silent waters, past obliteration. He showed her frozen stars and molten sun; she gave him long, entwined shadows and the sound of black velvet. He reached out to her and touched moss, grass, ancient trees, iridescent rocks; her fingertips, striving upwards, brushed old planets and silver moonlight, the flash of comets and the cry of dissolving suns.

They played games in which he died and she grew old; they did it for the sake of the joyous rebirth. They dissected time with love, and put it back together longer, better, slower. They invented toys out of mountains, plains, lakes, valleys. Their souls glistened like healthy fur.

They were lovers, they could conceive of nothing but love. But some things hated them. Dead stumps, barren eagles, stagnant ponds—these things resented their happiness. And certain urgencies of change ignored their declarations, indifferent to human intentions and content to continue their work of breaking down the universe. Certain conclusions, resistant to transformation, hastened to comply with ancient directives written on the bones, stenciled on the blood, tattooed on the inner side of the skin.

142

There was a bomb that needed explosion; there was a secret that required betrayal. And out of fear came knowledge, and sadness.

And one morning, Cathy was gone as if she had never been.

CHAPTER 23

GONE! CATHY WAS GONE! COULD IT BE POSSI-
ble? Could Life, that deadpan practical joker, be up to
his disastrous tricks again?

Marvin refused to believe it. He searched the confines
of the posada, and he poked patiently through the little
village beyond it. She was gone. He continued his search
in the nearby city of San Ramon de las Tristezas, and he
questioned waitresses, landlords, shopkeepers, whores,
policemen, pimps, beggars, and other inhabitants. He
asked if they had seen a girl fair as the dawn, with hair of
indescribable beauty, limbs of a previously unheard-of
felicity, features whose comeliness was matched only by
their harmony, etc. And those he questioned sadly replied, "Alas, señor, we have not seen thees woman, not
now or ever in our lives."

He calmed himself enough to give a coherent descrip-
tion, and found a road-mender who had seen a girl like
Cathy traveling west in a large automobile with a bulky,

cigar-smoking man. And a chimney sweep had spied her leaving town with her little gold and blue handbag. Her step had been firm. She had not looked back.

Then a gas-station attendant gave him a hastily scrawled note from Cathy that began, "Marvin dear, please try to understand and forgive me. As I tried to tell you so many times, it was necessary for me—"

The rest of the note was illegible. With the aid of a cryptanalyst, Marvin deciphered the closing words, which were: "But I shall always love you, and I hope you can find it in your heart to think of me occasionally with kindness. Your Loving Cathy."

The rest of the note, made enigmatic by grief, was insusceptible to human analysis.

To describe Marvin's emotion would be like trying to describe the dawn flight of the heron: both are ineffable and unspeakable. Suffice it to say that Marvin considered suicide, but decided against it, since it seemed entirely too superficial a gesture.

Nothing was enough. Intoxication was merely maudlin, and renunciation of the world seemed no more than the act of a peevish child. Because of the inadequacy of the attitudes open to him, Marvin struck none. Dry-eyed and zombie-like he moved through his days and nights. He walked, he talked, he even smiled. He was unfailingly polite. But it seemed to his dear friend Valdez that the real Marvin had vanished in an instantaneous explosion of sorrow, and that in his place there walked a poorly modeled representation of a man. Marvin was gone; the ringer who moved in his place looked as if, in its unfailing mimicry of humanness, it might collapse at any moment from strain.

146

Valdez was both perplexed and dismayed. Never had the wily old Master of Searches seen such a difficult case. With desperate energy he tried to rally his friend out of his living death.

He tried sympathy: "I know exactly how you feel, my unfortunate companion, for once, when I was quite a young man, I had quite a comparable experience, and I found—"

That did nothing, so Valdez tried brutality: "Christ damn me for a winnieburne, but are ye still mawking abaht after that bit of fluff wot walked out on yer? Now by God's wounds, I tell thee this: there's women past counting in this world of ours, and the man's no man who'd curl himself up in the corner when there's good lovin' to be had without . . ."

No response. Valdez tried eccentric distraction:

"Look, look over there, I see three birds on a limb, and one has a knife thrust through its throat and a scepter clutched in its claw, and yet it sings more merrily than the others! What do you make of it, eh?"

Marvin made nothing of it. Undismayed, Valdez tried to rouse his friend by piteous self-referral.

"Well, Marvin, lad, the medics have taken a look at that skin rash of mine and it seems that it's a case of pandemic impetigo. They give me 12 hours on the outside, after that I cash in my chips and make room for another man at the table. But for my last 12 hours, what I'd like to do is—"

Nothing. Valdez attempt to stir his friend with peasant philosophy:

"The simple farmers know best, Marvin. Do you know what they say? They say that a broken knife makes a

147

poor walking-stick. I think you should bear that in mind, Marvin. . . ."

But Marvin absentmindedly did not bear it in mind. Valdez swung to Hyperstrasian Ethics as expressed in the Timomachaean Scroll:

"Thou considerest thyself wounded, then? But consider: Self is Ineffable and Unitary, and not Susceptible to Externalities. Therefore it is merely a *Wound* which was *Wounded;* and this, being External to the Person and Extraneous to the Insight affords no cause for the Implication of Pain."

Marvin was not swayed by this argument. Valdez turned to psychology:

"Loss of the Beloved, according to Steinmetzer, is a ritual reenactment of the loss of the Fecal Self. Therefore, amusingly enough, when we think we mourn the dear departed, we actually are grieving the irreparable loss of our feces."

But this, too, could not penetrate Marvin's close-held passivity. His melancholic detachment from all human values seemed irrevocable; and this impression was heightened when, one quiet afternoon, his nose ring stopped ticking. It was not a bomb at all; it was merely a warning from Marduk Kras's constituents. And thus Marvin no longer stood in imminent danger of having his head blown off.

But even this stroke of good fortune did nothing to alter his gray robotic spirits. Quite unmoved, he noted the fact of his salvation as one might observe the passing of a cloud from the face of the sun.

Nothing seemed to have any effect upon him. And

even the patient Valdez was finally led to explain: "Marvin, you are a goddamned pain in the ass!"

Yet Marvin persevered, unmoved. And it seemed to Valdez and to the good people of San Ramon that this man was beyond human recall.

And yet, how little we know of the twists and turns of the human mind! For the very next day, contrary to all reasonable expectation, an event occurred that broke at last through Marvin's reserve, and inadvertently threw wide the floodgates of susceptibility behind which he had been hiding.

A single event! (Though it was in itself the beginning of yet another chain of causality—the quiet opening move in yet another of the uncountable dramas of the universe.)

It began, absurdly enough, with a man's asking Marvin for the time.

CHAPTER 24

THE EVENT OCCURRED ON THE NORTHERN side of the Plaza de los Muertos, shortly after the evening paseo and a full fifteen minutes before matins. Marvin had been taking his customary walk, past the statue of Jose Grimuchio, past the row of bootblacks gathered near the fifteenth-century pewter railing, to the fountain of San Briosci at the eastern corner of the grim little park. He had come even with the Tomb of the Misbegotten when a man stepped into his path and raised an imperious hand.

"A thousand pardons," the man said. "This unsolicited interruption of your solitude is regrettable to me, and perhaps offensive to you; yet still it is incumbent upon me to ask if by chance you could tell me the correct time?"

A harmless enough request—on the surface. Yet the man's appearance belied his commonplace words. He was of medium height and slight build, and he wore a

151

moustache of outmoded design, of a sort that can be seen in the Grier portrait of King Morquavio Redondo. His clothes were tattered but very clean and neatly pressed, and his cracked shoes were highly polished. On his right forefinger was an ornate signet ring of massy gold; his eyes were the cold hawk eyes of a man used to command.

His question concerning the time would have been commonplace had there not been clocks facing the plaza, and disagreeing in their separate computations by no more than three minutes.

Marvin answered the man with his usual unfailing politeness, glancing at his ankle watch and announcing the time as just five past the hour.

"Thank you, sir, you are most obliging," the man said. "Five past already? Time devours our feeble mortality, leaving us with but the sour residue of memory."

Marvin nodded. "Yet this ineffable and ungraspable quantity," he replied, "this time which no man may possess, is in truth our only possession."

The man nodded as though Marvin had said something profound, instead of merely voicing a well-mannered conversational commonplace. The stranger bent forward into a sweeping bow (more to be seen in a bygone day than in this plebian age of ours). In so doing he lost his balance and would have fallen had not Marvin grasped him strongly and set him upon his feet.

"Many thanks," the man said, never for a moment losing his poise. "Your grasp of time and of men is most sure; this shall not be forgotten."

And with that he whirled and marched away into the crowd.

Marvin watched him go, faintly perplexed. Something

152

about the fellow had not rung true. Perhaps it was the moustache, patently false, or the thickly penciled eyebrows, or the artificial wart on the left cheek; or perhaps it was the shoes, which had given an extra three inches to the man's height, or the cloak, which had been padded to augment the natural narrowness of the shoulders. Whatever it was, Marvin found himself bemused, but not immediately distrustful; for beneath the man's rodomontade there had been evidence of a cheerful and sturdy spirit not lightly to be discounted.

It was while thinking of these things that Marvin happened, by chance, to glance down at his right hand. Looking more closely, he saw a piece of paper in the palm. It certainly had not come there by natural means. He realized that the cloaked stranger must have pressed it upon him while stumbling (or, as Marvin realized now, while *pretending* to stumble).

This cast the events of the past few minutes into an entirely different light. Frowning slightly, Marvin unfolded the paper and read:

If the sir would care to hear something of interest and advantage both to himself and to the universe, the importance of which both the immediate present and in the far-flung future cannot be stressed too greatly, and which cannot be expatiated upon in this note in any detail for obvious and all-too-sufficient reasons, but which *shall be* revealed in due course assuming a commonality of interests and of ethical considerations, then let the sir proceed at the ninth hour to the Inn of the Hanged Man, and there let him take table in the far left-hand corner near the paired embrochures, and let him wear a white rosebud in his lapel and carry in his right hand a copy of the *Diario de Celsus* (4-star edition), and let him tap upon the table with the little finger of his right hand, in no particular rhythm.

These instructions being followed, One will come to you and make you acquainted with that which we believe you would like to hear.

[signed] One Who Wishes You Well.

Marvin mused for a considerable time upon that note and its implications. He sensed that in some unimaginable fashion a group of interrelated lives and problems, hitherto unknown to him, had crossed his path.

But now was the moment when he could choose. Did he really care to involve himself in anyone's scheme, no matter how noteworthy? Might it not be best to avoid involvement and pursue his own solitary way through the metaphoric deformations of the world?

Perhaps . . . yet still, the incident had intrigued him and offered an apparently inconsequential diversion to help him forget the pain of Cathy's loss. (Thus action serves as anodyne, whereas contemplation is revealed as the most direct form of involvement, and therefore much shunned by men.)

Marvin followed the instructions given to him in the note from the mysterious stranger. He bought a copy of the *Diario de Celsus* (4-star edition), and procured a white rosebud for his lapel. And at nine o'clock sharp he went to the Inn of the Hanged Man and sat down at the table in the far left-hand corner, near the paired embrochures. His heart was beating with some rapidity. It was not an entirely unpleasant sensation.

CHAPTER 25

THE INN OF THE HANGED MAN WAS A LOW yet cheerful place, and its clientele was composed, for the most part, of hearty specimens of the lower classes. Husky fish peddlers bawled for drink, and inflamed agitators howled abuse at the government and were hooted down by the heavy-thewed blacksmiths. A six-legged thorasorous was roasting in the great fireplace, and a scully basted the crackling carcass with honeyed juices. A fiddler had gotten up on a table and was playing a jig; his wooden leg rattled merrily in time with the old refrain. A drunken strumpet, with jeweled eyelids and artificial septum, wept in a corner with maudlin self-pity.

A perfumed dandy swept a lace handkerchief to his nose and threw a disdainful coin to the tightrope wrestlers. Farther to the left, at the common table, a bootblack reached into the pot for a morsel of scrag, and found his hand skewered to the table by the poniard of a riisman. This exploit was greeted with cheers by the assembled.

"Gawd save 'ee, sir, and whut'll thee be drunking?"

Marvin looked up and saw a waitress with red cheeks and extensive bosom waiting for his order.

"Mead, and it so please you," Marvin answered quietly.

"Ay, that we do be havin'," the girl replied. She bent to adjust her garter and whispered to Marvin, "Lawks, sir, do be mindful of yourself in this place which is in truth no fitten for a young gentleman such as thyself."

"Thanks for your warning," Marvin replied, "but if it comes to the rub, I hope that I may be allowed to believe that I might not be entirely unavailing."

"Ah, ye don't know them as is 'ere," the girl replied; and then moved away hastily, for a large gentleman dressed entirely in black had approached Marvin's table.

"Now by the sweet bleeding wounds of the Almighty and what have we here?" he shouted.

A silence fell over the inn. Marvin looked steadily upon the man, and recognized in his huge expanse of chest and abnormal reach that one whom people called "Black Denis." And he remembered the man's reputation as a ripper and tearer and general bully and spoiler.

Marvin affected not to notice the man's sweaty proximity. Instead, he took out a fan and wafted it gently in front of his nose.

The crowd roared with peasant mirth. Black Denis took a half step closer. Muscles along his arm writhed like cobras in travail as his fingers closed on the gaunt handle of his rapier.

"Damn me blind for a turnip-filler!" Black Denis

shouted, "but it seems most marvelous to me that we have here in our midst a fellow who looks most exceedingly like a king's spy!"

Marvin suspected that the man was trying to provoke him. Therefore he ignored the sally and buffed his fingernails with a tiny silver file.

"Well, slash me up the middle and tie me guts for a sash!" Black Denis swore. "It seems that some so-called gentlemun ain't no gentlemun at all since they don't acknowledge when another gentlemun is speaking at um. But maybe um's deaf, which I shall find out by examining the fellow's left ear—at home, at my leisure."

"Were you addressing me?" Marvin asked, in a suspiciously mild voice.

"Indeed I was," Black Denis said. "For it came to me of a sudden that me likes not your face."

"Indeed?" Marvin lisped.

"Aye!" thundered Black Denis. "Nor like I more your manner, nor the stench of your perfume, nor the shape of your foot nor the curve of your arm."

Marvin's glance narrowed. The moment was filled with murderous tension, and no sound could be heard save Black Denis's stertorous breathing. Then, before Marvin could reply, a man had run to Black Denis's side. It was a little hunchback who thus rashly interfered, a sallow man with a great white beard, standing no more than three feet high and dragging a club foot behind him.

"Ah, come now," the hunchback said to Black Denis. "Wilt shed blood on St. Origen's Eve, and it unworthy of your lordship's attention? For shame, Black Denis!"

"I'll shed blood an I so please, by the cankers of the holy red mountain!" swore the bully.

"Ay, spill his guts for him!" shouted a spindly, long-nosed fellow from the crowd, blinking with one blue eye and squinting with one brown.

"Ay, spill it!" a dozen other voices roared, taking up the cry.

"Gentlemen, please!" said the fat innkeeper, wringing his hands.

" 'E ain't never bothered you!" said the frowsy barmaid, a tray of glasses trembling in her hand.

"Nay, leave the popinjay to his drink," said the hunchback, tugging at Black Denis's sleeve and drooling from one side of his mouth.

"Unhand me, lump-shoulder!" Black Denis shouted, and struck out with a right hand the size of a padding mauler. It caught the little hunchback fair across the chest and propelled him across the room, driving him completely across the aleyard table until he fetched up against the cinch rack with a great clatter of broken glass.

"Now, by the maggots of eternity!" the huge brawler said, turning to Marvin.

Still Marvin fanned himself and sat back in his chair, relaxed but with eyes slightly narrowed. A more observant man might have noticed the faint anticipatory tremor along his thighs, the merest suggestion of flexion in his wrists.

Now he deigned to notice his molester. "Still here?" he queried. "Fellow, your importunities grow wearisome to the ear and redundant to the senses."

"Yeah?" Black Denis cried.

"Yeah," Marvin replied ironically. "Reiteration is ever the emphasis of the disingenuous; yet it amuses not my

158

fancy. Therefore remove yourself, fellow, and take your overheated carcass somewhere else, lest I cool it for thee by a bloodletting which any chirurgeon might envy."

Black Denis gaped at the effrontery of this deadly quiet insult. Then, with a speed which belied his bulk, he swept out his sword and brought it down in a stroke that cleaved the heavy oak table in two, and would have most assuredly done for Marvin had he not moved nimbly out of the way.

Bellowing with rage, Denis charged, swinging his sword like a windmill gone berserk. And Marvin danced lightly back, folded his fan, tucked it away in his belt, rolled up his sleeves, bent low to evade another stroke, leaped backward over a cedar table, and plucked up a carving knife. Then, gripping the knife lightly in his hand, he moved forward on gliding steps to do combat.

"Take flight, sir!" the barmaid cried. "He'll split 'ee, and 'ee with naught but a tinysome table steel in 'ee's hand and it with no great edge on it!"

"Take care, young man!" the hunchback cried, taking refuge beneath a hanging side of bartels.

"Spill his guts for him!" the spindly, long-nosed fellow with the piebald eyes cried.

"Gentlemen, please!" cried the unhappy landlord.

The two combatants were met now in the center of the common room, and Black Denis, his face twisted with passion, feinted and swung a cutlass stroke powerful enough to split an oak. Marvin moved with deadly sureness inside of the blow, deflecting it with his knife in *quatre,* and immediately riposting in *quinze.* This deft counter was blocked only by the abnormal swiftness of

Denis's *revanche,* else it would surely have cut the gullet out of the man.

Black Denis came back onto guard, looking upon his opponent with more than a suggestion of respect. Then he roared with berserker rage, and drove forward into the attack, forcing Marvin back across the smoky room.

"A double Napoleon on the big fellow!" cried the perfumed dandy.

"Done!" cried the hunchback. "That slender lad has the footwork, mark it well."

"Footwork ne'er stopped swinging steel e'er now," the dandy lisped. "Wilt back thy judgment with thy purse?"

"Ay! I'll add five Louis d'Or!" said the hunchback, fumbling for his purse.

And now others in the crowd had caught the gaming fever. "Ten rupees on the Denis!" shouted the long-nosed fellow. "Nay, I'll offer odds of three to one!"

"Make it four to one!" cried the ever-cautious landlord, "and seven to five on first blood!" And so saying, he swept out a bag of gold sovereigns.

"Done!" screamed the piebald-eyed fellow, putting up three silver talents and a gold half-denarius. "And by the Black Mother, I'll even offer eight to six on a chest-cut!"

"I'll take the bet!" shrieked the barmaid, taking a bag of Maria Theresa thalers out of her bosom. "And I'll give you six-five pick 'em on first amputation!"

"I'll take that!" the perfumed dandy shrilled. "And by my wattles, I'll even offer nine to four that the slender lad runs out of here like a scorched grayhound before third blood!"

"I'll take that bet," Marvin Flynn said, with an amused

160

smile. Evading Denis's clumsy rush he plucked a bag of florins out of his sash and threw it to the dandy. Then he settled down seriously to fight.

Even in these few brief moves, Marvin's skill at fence could clearly be seen. Yet he was faced with a powerful and determined opponent, who wielded a sword many times larger than Marvin's inadequate weapon, and who seemed determined to the point of madness.

The attack came, and all in the crowd except for the hunchback held their breaths as Black Denis rushed down like an incarnation of Juggernaut. Before that impetuous rush, Marvin was forced to give ground. He backed away, vaulted over a table, found himself wedged into a corner, leaped high and caught the chandelier, swung across the room and dropped lightly to his feet.

Bewildered, and perhaps feeling a shade unsure of himself, Black Denis resorted to a trick. As they came together again, Denis's long arm swept a chair into Marvin's path; and as Marvin dodged, Denis grasped a collard of black Ignean pepper from a table and flung it into Marvin's face. . . .

But Marvin's face was no longer there. Pivoting and driving off his left foot, Marvin evaded the treacherous tactic. He feinted low with his knife, double-feinted with his eyes, and executed a perfect stepback crossover.

Black Denis blinked stupidly and looked down to see the handle of Marvin's knife jutting from his chest. His eyes opened wide in astonishment, and his sword hand came swinging up to the riposte.

Marvin turned serenely on his heel and walked slowly away, leaving his unprotected back exposed to the glint-edged cutlass!

161

Black Denis began his downward swing; but already a thin gray film had formed over his eyes. Marvin had judged the severity of the wound with exquisite precision, for Black Denis's sword clattered to the floor, to be joined a moment later by the great body of the brawler.

Without looking back, Marvin crossed the room and regained his chair. He opened his fan; then, frowning, he slipped a lace handkerchief out of his pocket and dabbled at his forehead. Two or three drops of perspiration marred its marble perfection. Flynn wiped the drops away, then threw away the handkerchief.

The room was in absolute silence. Even the piebald-eyed man had stopped his stertorous breathing.

It was perhaps the most amazing exhibit of swordsmanship that the inhabitants had ever seen. Brawlers one and all, and calling no man master, still they were impressed.

A moment later, pandemonium broke loose. All crowded around Marvin, cheering and exclaming, and marveling at the skill he had shown with pointed steel. The two rope wrestlers (brothers, born deaf-mutes) made squealing noises and turned somersaults; the hunchback grinned and counted his winnings with foam-flecked lips; the barmaid looked at Marvin with an embarrassing excess of ardor; the proprietor gruffly served drinks on the house; the piebald-eyed man snuffled through his long nose and talked about luck; even the perfumed dandy was moved to offer perfunctory congratulations.

Slowly the room returned to normal. Two bull-necked servitors dragged out Black Denis's body, and the fickle crowd pelted the corpse with orange peels. The roast was set again to turning on the spit, and the rattle of dice and swish of cards could be heard over the playing of the blind, one-legged fiddler.

The dandy strolled over to Marvin's table and looked down upon him, hand on hip and feathered hat akimbo. " 'Pon my honor, sir," the dandy said, "you do indeed have some qualifications at fence; and it seems to me that your skills could be rewarded in the service of the Cardinal Macchurchi, who is always on the lookout for apt and agile fellows."

"I am not for hire," Marvin said quietly.

"I am glad to hear it," the dandy said. And now, looking at the man more closely, Marvin perceived a white rosebud in his buttonhole, and a copy of the *Diario de Celsus* (4-star edition) in his hand.

The dandy's eyes flashed a warning. In his most effete voice, he said, "Well then, sir, my congratulations again; and perhaps, if you would care for a bit of sport, you will join me in my chambers on the Avenue of Martyrs. We could discuss the finer points of swordplay, and drink a rather adequate little wine which has lain in my family's vaults for 103 years, and perhaps even hazard another topic or two of mutual interest."

Now Marvin was able to recognize, beneath his disguise, the man who had pressed a note into his hand earlier.

"Sir," Marvin said, "your invitation does me honor."

"Not at all, sir. Your acknowledgment of my invitation does me honor."

"Nay, sir," Marvin insisted, and would have examined the honor question further had not the man cut short the punctilio and whispered, "We'll leave at once, then.

163

Black Denis was but a harbinger—a straw to show us which way the wind blows. And I greatly fear, lest we get ourselves promptly hence, it may well blow us a hurricane."

"That would be most unfortunate," Marvin said, grinning very slightly.

"Landlord! Set this upon my account!"

"Ay, Sir Gules," the landlord replied, bowing low.

And so they went out together into the fog-bound night.

CHAPTER 26

THROUGH THE TORTUOUS LANES OF THE central city they went, past the grim iron-gray walls of the Terc Fortress, past the infamous Spodney Asylum, wherein the screams of abused madmen mingled strangely with the squeak of the great waterwheel at Battlegrave Landing; past the howling of prisoners in the squat and ominous Donjon of the Moon, and then past the malodorous High Battlement with its grisly row of spiked torsos.

Being men of their time and age, neither Marvin nor Sir Gules gave notice to these sounds and sights. Quite unmoved they walked past the Garbage Pond wherein the former regent had gratified his mad nocturnal fancies; and without a glance they went by Lion's Gambit, where petty debtors and child malefactors were buried headfirst in quick-setting cement as an example to others.

It was a hard age, and some might consider it a cruel age. Manners were refined, but passions ran unchecked.

The most exquisite punctilio was observed; but death by torture was the common lot of most. It was an age in which six out of seven women died in childbirth; in which infant mortality was a shocking 87 percent; in which the average life-expectancy was no more than 12.3 years; in which the Plague yearly ravaged the central city, carrying away an estimated two-thirds of the population; in which continual religious warfare halved the able-bodied male population every year—to the point where some regiments were forced to use blind men as gunnery officers.

And yet, it could not be considered an unhappy age. Despite difficulties, the population soared to new heights every year, and men aspired to fresh extremes of audacity. If life was uncertain, it was at least interesting. Machinery had not bred individual initiative out of the race as yet. And though there were shocking class differences and feudal privilege reigned supreme, checked only by the dubious power of the king and the baleful presence of the clergy, still it could fairly be called a democratic age and a time of individual opportunity.

But neither Marvin nor Sir Gules were thinking of these things as they approached a narrow old house with drawn shutters and a brace of horses posted near the door. They were not contemplating individual enterprise, though indeed they were engaged in it; nor did they consider death, though it surrounded them constantly. Theirs was not a self-conscious age.

"Well then," Sir Gules said, leading his guest down the carpeted floor past the silent manservants to a high wainscoted room in which a cheery fire snapped and crackled in the great onyx fireplace.

166

Marvin did not answer. His eye was taking in the details of the room. The carven armoire was surely tenth century, and the portrait on the west wall, half-hidden by its gilt frame, was a genuine Moussault.

"Come, sit, I pray thee," said Sir Gules, sinking gracefully to a David Ogilvy half-couch decorated in the Afghan brocade so popular that year.

"Thank you," Marvin said, sitting upon an eight-legged John IV with rosewood handles and a backing of heart-o'-palm.

"A little wine?" Sir Gules said, handling with casual reverence the bronze decanter with gold chasings engraved by Dagobert of Hoyys.

"Not just at the moment, give thee thanks," Marvin replied, brushing a fleck of dust from his stuff-colored outercoat of green baptiste with lisle froggings, made to his measure by Geoffrey of Palping Lane.

"Then mayhap a touch of snuff?" Sir Gules enquired, proferring his small platinum snuffbox made by Durr of Snedum, upon which was portrayed in steel-point a hunting scene from the Orange Forest of Lesh.

"Perhaps later," Marvin said, squinting down at the double-furled silver thread laces on his dancing pumps.

"My purpose in bringing you here," his host said abruptly, "was to enquire as to the availability of your aid to a cause both good and righteous, and with which you are not, I believe, entirely unacquainted. I refer to the Sieur Lamprey Height d'Augustin, better known as The Enlightened."

"D'Augustin!" Marvin exclaimed. "Why, I knew him when I was little more than a lad, in '02 or '03, the year of the Speckled Plague! Why, he used to visit at our chalet! I can still remember the marzipan apples he used to bring me!"

"I thought you would remember him," Gules said quietly. "All of us do."

"And how is that great and good gentleman?"

"Well enough—we hope."

Marvin was instantly alert. "Your meaning, sir?"

"Last year, d'Augustin was working on his country estate at Duvannemor, which is just beyond Moueur d'Alençon in the foothills of the Sangrela."

"I know the place," Marvin said.

"He was finishing his masterwork, *The Ethics of Indecision*, with which he has travailed himself these past twenty years. When suddenly, a host of armed men burst into the Rune Study where he was working, having overpowered his servants and bribed his personal bodyguard. No one else was present save his daughter, who was helpless to interfere. These nameless men seized and bound d'Augustin, burned all extant copies of his book, and took him away."

"Infamous!" cried Marvin.

"His daughter, witnessing so horrid a sight, swooned away into a lassitude so complete that it resembled death; and thus, through an inadvertent counterfeit, she was spared from death itself."

"Shocking!" muttered Marvin. "But who would let slip violence upon a harmless cribbler whom many call the outstanding philosopher of our day and age?"

"Harmless, say thee?" Sir Gules enquired, his lips quirking into a painful grimace. "Are you then acquainted with d'Augustin's work that you say so?"

"I have had not the privilege of acquaintance," Marvin

said. "My life, in truth, has availed me little opportunity for such matters, since I have been traveling continually for somesuch time now. But I thought that the writings of so gentle and esteemed a man would surely—"

"I beg to differ," Sir Gules said. "This fine and upright old man whom we are discussing has been led, by an irreversible process of Logical Inductiveness, to put forth certain doctrines which, if they were popularly known, might well cause bloody revolution."

"That scarce seems a goodly matter," Marvin replied coldly. "Wouldst teach me damnable sedition?"

"Nay, softly, softly! These doctrines which d'Augustin proclaims are not so shocking in themselves, but rather, in their consequences. That is to say, they take on the timbre of Moral Facticity, and are no more truly seditious than is the monthly wax and wane of th' moon."

"Well ... give me an example," Marvin said.

"D'Augustin proclaims that men are born free," Gules said softly.

Marvin thought about that. "A new-fangled notion," he declared at last, "but not without its suasion. Tell me more."

"He declares that upright conduct is meritorious and pleasing in the eyes of God."

"A strange way of looking at things," Marvin decided. "And yet—hmmm."

"He also holds that the unexamined life is not worth living."

"Quite a radical point of view," Marvin said. "And it is, of course, obvious what would happen were these statements to fall into the hands of the populace at large. The

169

authority of king and church would inevitably be undermined . . . and yet—and yet—"

"Yes?" Gules prompted softly.

"And yet," Marvin said, gazing dreamily at the terracotta ceiling with its inscriblature of interlocked palladiums, "and yet might not a new order arise out of the chaos which would unerringly ensue? Might not a new world be born in which the overweening humours of the nobility would be checked and ameliorated by the concept of personal worth, and in which the thundering threats of a church gone base and political would be countered by a new relationship between a man and his God unmediated by fat priest or larcenous friar?"

"Do you really think that is possible?" Gules asked, in a voice like silk sliding over velvet.

"Yes," Marvin said. "Yes, by the hangnails of God, I so do believe! And I will aid you in rescuing d'Augustin and in disseminating this strange and revolutionary new doctrine!"

"Thank you," Gules said simply. And he made a gesture with his hand.

A figure glided out from behind Marvin's chair. It was the hunchback. Marvin caught the deadly wink of steel as the creature sheathed his knife.

"No insult intended," Gules said earnestly. "We were sure of you, of course. But had you found our plan repugnant, it would have been incumbent upon us to hide our poor judgment in an unmarked grave."

"The precaution lends point to your story," Marvin said dryly. "But me likes it not such keen appreciation."

"Such confabulation is our common lot in life," the hunchback quoth. "And indeed, did not the Greeks con-

170

sider it better to die in the hands of friends than to languish in the claws of enemies? Our roles are chosen for us in this world by the stern dictates of an unrelenting Fate; and many a man who thought to play the emperor on Life's stage found himself cast for a corpse instead."

"Sir," said Marvin, "you sound to me a man who has experienced some casting problems himself."

"One well might say so," the hunchback replied dryly. "I would not of myself have selected this lowly part, had not exigencies beyond prediction forced me to it."

So saying, the hunchback reached down and unstrapped his legs, which had been bound to his thighs, and thereby rose to his full height of six feet one. He unfastened the hump from his back, wiped greasepaint and drool from his face, combed his hair, detached his beard and his club foot, then turned to Marvin with a wry smile upon his face.

Marvin stared at this man transformed; then bowed low and exclaimed, "Milord Inglenook bar na Idrisi-san, first lord of the Admiralty, Familiar to the Prime Minister, Advisor Extraordinary to the King, Bludgeon of the Church Rampant and Invocateur of the Grand Council!"

"I am that person," Inglenook responded. "And I play the hunchback for reasons most politic; for were my presence even suspected here by my rival, Lord Blackamoor de Mordevund, all of us would be dead men ere the frogs in the Pond Royal had chance to croak at first ray of Phoebus!"

"This ivy of conspiracy doth grow on high towers," Marvin commented. "I surely will serve you and God give me strength, unless some tavern brawler lets light into my belly with a yard of steel."

171

"If you refer to the incident of Black Denis," Sir Gules said, "I can assure you that the matter was staged for the eyes of whatever spies Sir Blackamoor might have set upon us. In actuality, Black Denis was one of us."

"Wonder upon wonders!" Marvin declared. "This octopus, it seems, has many tentacles. But gentlemen, it wonders me why, of all puissant gentlemen in this our kingdom, you sought out one who boasts no special privilege nor high position nor monetary wealth nor nothing save the title of gentlemen under God and lord of his own honor and bearer of a thousand-year-old name."

"You are reckless in your modesty!" Lord Inglenook laughed. "For it is known among all that your skill in the fenceyard is unsurpassed, except perhaps for the wily swordplay of the detestable Blackamoor."

"I am but a student of the steely art," Marvin replied carelessly. "Yet still, if my poor gift will serve you, sobeit. And now, gentlemen, what would you of me?"

"Our plan," Inglenook said slowly, "has the virtue of great daring, and the defect of immense danger. A single cast of the dice wins all, or loses us the wager of our lives. A grave gamble! And yet, methinks you would not like not this hazard."

Marvin smiled while construing the sentence, then said, "A quick game is ever a lively one."

"Excellent!" breathed Gules, rising to his feet. "We must take ourselves now to Castelgatt in the valley of the Romaine. And during the ride there, we shall acquaint you with the details of our scheme."

And so it was that, muffled in their greatcloaks, the three departed the high narrow house by the dormer stairwell, walking past the chain locker to the postern

172

gate by the old west wall. Here, posted and waiting, was a coach and four, with two armed guards mounted on the slackrails.

Marvin made to enter the coach and saw a person already within. It was a girl; and peering more closely, he saw—

"Cathy!" he cried.

She looked at him without comprehension, and answered in a cold, imperious voice, "Sir, I am Catarina d'Augustin, and I know not your face nor like I your style of presumed familiarity."

There was no recognition in her beautiful gray eyes, and no time to ask questions. For even as Sir Gules made hasty introductions, a shout could be heard behind them.

"You there, in the coach! Halt in the name of the King!"

Glancing back, Marvin could see a captain of dragoons with ten mounted men behind him.

"Treachery!" shouted Inglenook. "Quick, coachmen, let us away!"

With a clatter of traces and a rattle of bits, the four matched stallions propelled the coach down the narrow alley in the direction of Ninestones and Oceansideways High Road.

"Can they overtake us?" asked Marvin.

"Mayhap," Inglenook said. "They seem damnably well mounted, damn their blue blistered backsides! Your pardon, madame. . . ."

For a few moments Inglenook watched the horsemen clatter along not twenty yards behind, their sabers glittering in the dim lamplight. Then he shrugged and turned away.

173

"Let me inquire," Inglenook inquired, "as to whether you are conversant with recent political developments here and elsewhere in the Old Empire; for this knowledge is needful to make intelligible to you the necessity for the particular form and moment of our scheme."

"I fear that my political knowledge is but indifferent poor," Marvin said.

"Then permit me to relate to you a few details of the background, which will render the situation and its import more malleable to the intelligence."

Marvin settled back, hearing the drumming of the dragoon's horses in his ears. Cathy, seated opposite him and slightly to his right, stared coldly at the swinging tassels on Sir Gules' hat. And Lord Inglenook began to speak:—

CHAPTER 27

"*THE OLD KING DIED LESS THAN A DECADE*
ago, at the full flood of the Suessian heresy, leaving no
clear successor to the throne of Mulvavia. Thus, the passions of a troubled continent came ominously to the
boil.

"Three claimants jostled for the Butterfly Throne.
Prince Moroway of Theme held the Patent Obvious,
which had been awarded him by a bribed but still official
Council of Electionate. And if that were not sufficient, he
held as well by the doctrine of Regal Empleatude, since
he was the acknowledged, illegitimate second (and only
surviving) son of Baron Norway, the old king's sister's
half-cousin through the powerful Mortjoys of Danat.

"In less troubled times, this might have been sufficient. But for a continent on the verge of civil and religious war, there were defects in the claim, and even more in
the claimant.

"Prince Moroway was merely eight years old and had

never been known to utter a word. According to the portrait by Mouvey, he had a monstrously swollen head, a slack jaw, and the unfocused eyes of a hydrocephalic idiot. His only known pleasure was his collection of worms (the finest on the continent).

"His main opposition for the succession was Gottlieb Hosstratter, Duke of Mela and Receiptor-in-Ordinary of the Imperial Marginland, whose dubious bloodlines were backed by the schismatic Suessian Hierarchy, and most particularly by the enfeebled Hierarch of Dodessa.

"A second claimant, Romrugo of Vars, might have been discounted were it not that he backed his petition with a force of fifty thousand battle-hardened troopers from the southern principality of Vask. Young and vigorous, Romrugo had a reputation for eccentricity; his marriage to his favorite mare Orsilla, was condemned by the orthodox Owensian clergy of which he was the absent-minded champion. Nor did he win favor among the burghers of Gint-Loseine, whose proud city he ordered buried under twenty feet of earth "as a gift to future archaeologists." Yet withal, his claim to the throne of Mulvavia might have been speedily legitimized had he possessed the wherewithal with which to pay his fighting men.

"Unfortunately for Romrugo, he had no personal fortune. (It had been squandered upon the purchase of the Lethertean scrolls.) Therefore, in order to raise his army's payroll, he proposed an alliance with the wealthy but ineffectual Free City of Tihurrue, which commanded the straits of Sidue.

"This unthinking move brought down upon his head the wrath of the Duchy of Puls, whose western frontier

176

had long guarded the exposed flank of the Old Empire from the depradations of the pagan Monogoths. The stern, singleminded young grandduke of Puls immediately joined forces with the schismatic Hosstratter—surely as strange an alliance as the continent had ever seen—and thus became a direct menace to Prince Moroway, and to the Mortjoys of Danat who supported him. So, quite unexpectedly, finding himself surrounded on three sides by Suessians or their allies, and on the fourth side by the restive Monogoths, Romrugo began casting around desperately for a new alliance.

"He found it in the enigmatic figure of Baron Lord Darkmouth, Prepossessor of the Isle of Turplend. The tall and brooding Baron set to sea at once with a battle fleet of twenty-five galleons, and all Mulvavia held its breath as the ominous line of ships sailed down the Dorter and into the Escher Sea.

"Could the balance still have been preserved, even at this late hour? Perhaps, if Moroway had held firm to his former pledges to the Marche Cities. Or if the old Hierarch of Dodessa, contemplating at last the necessity of an accomodation with Hosstratter, had not chosen that inappropriate moment to die, and thus to give power to the epileptic Murvey of Hunfutmouth. Or if Red Hand Ericmouth, chief of the west Monogoths, had not chosen that moment to banish Propeia, sister of the stern Archduke of Puls, known as the "Hammer against Heretics" (by which he meant all who did not subscribe to his own narrowly orthodox Delongianism).

"But the hand of Fate intervened to stay the inevitable moment; for Baron Darkmouth's galleons were caught in the Great Storm of '03, and driven to take refuge at

177

Tihurrue, which they sacked, thus dissolving Romrugo's alliance before it was fairly underway, and causing revolt among the unpaid Vaskians of his army, who deserted by regiments and joined Hosstratter, whose lands lay closest to their line of march.

"Thus Hosstratter, third and most reluctant of the royal petitioners, who had become resigned to his loss, found himself back in the contest; and Moroway, whose star had glittered high, discovered that the Echilides Mountains were no protection when the eastern passes were held by a determined enemy.

"The man most affected by all of this, of course, was Romrugo. His position was unenviable: deserted by his troops, forsworn by his ally Baron Darkmouth (who had his hands full trying to hold Tihurrue against a determined attack by the pirates of the Rullish coast), and menaced even in his fiefdom of Vars by the long and deadly arm of Mortjoy's conspiracy, while the Marche Cities looked hungrily on. As capstone to his pillar of ill fortune, his mare Orsilla chose that moment to desert him.

"Yet even in the depths of adversity, the self-confident Romrugo did not falter. His mare's desertion was hailed by the frightened Owensian clergy, who granted their dubious champion a Divorce in Absolute, and then learned to their horror that the cynical Romrugo intended to use his freedom to wed Propeia and thus align himself with the grateful Archduke of Puls. . . .

"These were the factors that exercised men's passions in that fateful year. The continent stood poised upon the brink of catastrophe. Peasants buried their crops underground and sharpened their scythes. Armies stood to at-

178

tention and prepared to move in any direction. The turbulent mass of the West Monogoths, pressed from behind by the still more turbulent mass of hard-riding cannibal Allahuts, massed threateningly on the borders of the Old Empire.

"Darkmouth hastened to reequip his galleys, and Hosstratter paid the Vaskian troopers and trained them for a new kind of war. Romrugo cemented his new alliance with Puls, achieved a détente with Ericmouth, and took account of the new rivalry between Mortjoy and the epileptic but dourly able Murvey. And Moroway of Theme, unconscious ally of the Rullish pirates, unwilling champion of the Suessian heresy, and unwitting accomplice of Red Hand Ericmouth, looked to the grim eastern slopes of the Echilides and waited in trepidation.

"It was at this moment of supreme and universal tension that Milord d'Augustin all unwittingly chose to announce the imminent completion of his work of philosophy. . . ."

Inglenook's voice faded slowly away, and for a time there was no sound but the heavy thrum of horse's hooves. Then Marvin said quietly, "I understand now."

"I knew you would," Inglenook answered warmly. "And in light of this, you can understand our plan, which is to assemble at Castelgatt and then strike immediately."

Marvin nodded. "Under the circumstances there could be no other way."

"But first," Inglenook said, "we must rid ourselves of these pursuing dragoons."

"As to that," Marvin said, "I have a plan. . . ."

179

CHAPTER 28

BY A CLEVER RUSE, MARVIN AND HIS COM-
patriots were able to elude the pursuing dragoons and
to come unscathed into the great moated tiltyard of
Castelgatt. There, upon the sounding of the twelfth hour,
the conspirators were to assemble, make final disposi-
tions, and move out that very night for the audacious
attempt to rescue d'Augustin from the formidable grasp
of Blackamoor.

Marvin retired to his chambers in the high east wing,
and there shocked his page by insisting upon a basin of
water in which to wash his hands. It was considered a
strange affectation on his part in that age in which even
the greatest court ladies were accustomed to hide
smudges of dirt under perfumed gauze bandages. But
Marvin had picked up the custom during his stay among
the gay and pagan Tescos of the southern Remoueve,
whose soapy fountains and spongy sculpture were wonders of wonders to the complacent and grimy northern

nobility. And in spite of the laughter of his peers and the frowns of the clergy, Marvin stubbornly insisted that an occasional scrub of the hands did no damage, so long as the water touched no other part.

His ablutions completed, and clad only in black satin half-knickers, white lace shirt, cavalry boots and shoulder-length gloves of Eretzian chamois, and wearing only his sword Coueur de Stabbat, which had been handed down in his family father-to-son for five hundred years, Marvin heard a half-noise behind him and whirled, hand to hilt.

"La, sir, wouldst run me through with thy terrible great sword?" mocked the Lady Catarina—for it was she —standing just inside the paneled doorway to the inner chamber.

"Faith, your ladyship startled me," Marvin said. "But as for running thee through, that indeed I wouldst do right merrily, though not with sword but with a trustier weapon which it happens I do possess."

"Fie, sir," the Lady Catarina said mockingly. "Offerest violence to a lady?"

"Merely the violence of pleasure," Marvin replied gallantly.

"Your words are too glib by half," said the Lady Catarina. "I believe it has been noted that the longest and wiliest tongues conceal the shortest and least adequate of Weapons."

"Your ladyship does me injustice," Marvin said. "For I daresay my Weapon is eminently capable of the uses it may encounter, sharp enough to penetrate the best defence in the world, and durable enough for repeated stabbings. And, quite apart from such utilitarian uses, it

182

has learned from me certain infallible tricks, the which it would be my respectful pleasure to show your ladyship."

"Nay, keep your Weapon in its scabbard," the lady quoth, indignantly, but with sparkling eyes. "Me likes not the sound of 't; for braggart's steel is ever pliable tin, shiny to the eye yet damnably malleable to the touch."

"I beg of thee but to touch the edge and point," Marvin said, "and thus submit thy raillery to th' test of Usage."

She shook her pretty head. "Know, sir, that such Pragmatics are for graybeard philosophers with rheumy eyes; a lady relies upon her intuition."

"Lady, I worship thy intuition," Marvin responded.

"Why, sir, what wouldst Thou, the Prepossessor of a dubious Weapon of indetermined length and uncertain temper, know of a woman's intuition?"

"Lady, my heart tells me that it is exquisite and ineffable, and possessed of a pleasing shape and delicate fragrance, and that—"

"Enough, sir!" the Lady Catarina cried, blushing hotly and fanning herself furiously with a Japanese fan whose corrugated surface portrayed the Investiture of the Iichi.

Both fell silent. They had been conversing in the old language of Courtly Love, in which symbolic apostrophe played so important a part. In those days it was deemed no breach of the etiquette for even the best-bred and most demure of young ladies to thus converse; theirs was not a frightened age.

But now a shadow of seriousness had fallen over the two participants. Marvin glowered, fingering the gray steel buttons of his white lace shirt. And the Lady Catarina looked troubled. She wore a paneled gown of dove

183

tulip with slashings of chrome red; and, as was the custom, the neckline was cut fashionably low to reveal the firm rosy swelling of her little abdomen. Upon her feet were sandal-pumps of ivory-colored damask; and her hair, piled high upon a jade ratouelle, was adorned with a garland of spring snippinies. Never in his life had Marvin seen so beautiful a sight.

"Can we not cease this ceaseless play of word-foolery?" Marvin asked quietly. "May we not say that which is in our hearts, 'stead of fencing thus with heartless ingenuities?"

"I dare not!" the Lady Catarina murmured.

"And yet, you are Cathy, who loved me once in another time and place," Marvin said inexorably, "and who now plays me for the unacknowledged gallant."

"You must not speak of that which once had been," Cathy said, in a frightened whisper.

"Yet still you loved me once!" Marvin cried hotly. "Deny me this an you find it false!"

"Yes," she said in a failing voice, "I loved thee once."

"And now?"

"Alas!"

"But speak and tell me reason!"

"Nay, I cannot!"

"Will not, rather."

"As thee wish; the choice is servant to the heart."

"I would not have you believe that," she said softly.

"No? Then surely the desire is father to the intent," Marvin said, his face gone hard and pitiless. "And standing thus in familial relationship, not even the wisest of men would deny that Love is inbonded to its half-sister

184

Indifference, and Faithfulness is thrall to the cruel step-mother, Pain."

"Can you so consider me?" she cried weakly.

"Why, Lady, you leave me choiceless," Marvin responded in a voice of ringing bronze. "And thus my barque of Passion is Derelict upon a Sea of Memory, blown off its rightful course by the fickle wind of Indifference, and driven toward the rockbound Coast of Agony by the inexorable Tide of Human Events."

"And yet, I would not have it thus," Catarina said, and Marvin thrilled to hear even so mild an affirmation of that which he had considered lost beyond recall.

"Cathy—"

"Nay, it cannot be," she cried, recoiling in evident agony, her color high and her abdomen rising and falling with the emotion within her. "You know not of the wretched circumstances of my situation."

"I demand to know!" Marvin cried, then whirled, his hand darting to his sword. For the great oaken door of his chamber had swung noiselessly open, and there, leaning negligently in the doorway, a man stood with arms folded over his chest and a half-smile playing across his thin, bearded lips.

"In faith! We are undone!" Catarina cried, her hand pressed to her trembling abdomen.

"Sir, what would thou?" Marvin asked hotly. "I demand to know thy name, and the reason for this most ungentle and unseemly investiture!"

"All shall be speedily revealed thee," the man in the doorway said, his voice revealing a faint and menacing lisp. "My name, sir, is Lord Blackamoor, 'gainst whom your puerile plans have been cast; and I have entered

185

this chamber from simple privilege of one who dutifully desires introduction to his wife's young friend."

"Wife?" Marvin echoed.

"This lady," Blackamoor declared, "who has the uncertain habit of not straightaways introducing herself, is indeed the Most Noble Catarina d'Augustin di Blackamoor, the most loving wife to this your humble servant."

And so saying, Blackamoor swept off his hat and louted low, then resumed his exquisite's pose in the doorway.

Marvin read the truth in Cathy's tear-stained eyes and shuddering abdomen. Cathy, his beloved Cathy, the wife of Blackamoor, the most detested enemy of those who espoused the cause of d'Augustin, who was Cathy's own father!

Yet there was no time to consider these strange propinquities of sensibility; for the foremost consideration was of Blackamoor himself, standing miraculously within a castle held by his enemies, and betraying no hint of nervousness at a position that should have been perilous in the extreme.

And this infallibly meant that the situation was not as Marvin had supposed it, and that the threads of destiny were tangled now past his immediate comprehension.

Blackamoor in Castelgatt? Marvin considered the implications, and a sensation of cold came over him, as though the angel of death had brushed past him with stygian wings.

Murder lurked in this room—but for whom? Marvin feared the worst, but turned quite steadily, his face a mask of obsidian, and faced the enemy who was his beloved's husband and the captor of her father.

186

CHAPTER 29

MILORD LAMPREY DI BLACKAMOOR STOOD silent and at his ease. He was above the middling height, and possessed a frame of extreme emaciation, punctuated by his narrow, closely cropped beard of jetty black, his deep-swept sideburns, and his hair cut *en brosse* and allowed to fall upon his forehead in snaky ringlets. And yet the appearance of narrowness was offset by the breadth of shoulder and the powerful swordsman's arm that could be glimpsed beneath his half-cloak of ermitage. He wore his points and josses in the new foppish style, interlaced with macedium pointings and relieved only by a triple row of crepe-silver darturs. His face was coldly handsome, marred only by a puckered scar that ran from his right temple to the left corner of his mouth, and which he had defiantly painted a fiery crimson. This lent to his sarcastic features a look both sinister and absurd.

"It would seem," Blackamoor drawled, "that we have

played this farce long enough. The denouement approaches."

"Does milord then have his third act prepared?" Marvin inquired steadily.

"The actors have been given their cues," Blackamoor said. Negligently he snapped his fingers.

Into the room walked Milord Inglenook, followed by Sir Gules and a platoon of sour-faced Thuringian soldiery in plain deal-colored half-jackets of buff, with sword-mattocks at the ready.

"What damnable entrapment is this?" Marvin demanded.

"Tell him—brother," Blackamoor mocked.

"Yes, it is true," Lord Inglenook said, his face ashen. "Blackamoor and I are half-brothers, since our common mother was the Marquesita Roseata of Timon, daughter to the Elector of Brandeis and sister-in-marriage to Longsword Silverblain, who was father to Red Sword Ericmouth, and whose first husband, Marquelle of the Marche, was father to me, but after whose decease wed Huntford, Bastard Royal of Cleve and Pretender to the Eleactiq Preserve."

"His outmoded sense of honor rendered him sensible to my scheme and ductile to the veriest suggestion," Blackamoor sneered.

"A strange state of affairs," Marvin mused, "when a man's honor dishonors a man."

Inglenook bent his head and said nothing.

"But as for you, Milady," Marvin said, addressing Cathy, "it mazes me past comprehension why you should choose marriage with the captivator of your father."

"Alas," Cathy said, "it is a most diverse and noisome

188

tale, for he courted me with threats and indifference, and captivated me by the dark power he doth possess which none oppose; and further, by the use of damnable drugs and double-edged words and sly skillful movements of his hands he did bemuse my sense to a state of counterfeit passion, wherein I seemed to swoon for touch of his damnable body and nibblature of his detestable lips. And since I was denied the comforts of religion during this period, and therefore had no way of knowing the true from the induced, I did indeed succumb. Nor do I offer any excuse of attenuation for myself."

Marvin turned to the man who was his last remaining hope. "Sir Gules!" he cried. "Put hand to sword and we shall yet hew our way to freedom!"

Blackamoor laughed dryly. "Think you he'll draw? Mayhap. But 'twill be but to peel an apple, or so I deem!"

Marvin stared into the face of his friend, and saw written there a shame deeper than steel and deadlier than poison.

"It is true," Sir Gules said, trying to keep his voice steady. "I cannot aid thee, though my heart breaks at your plight."

"What damnable sorcery has Blackamoor rendered upon you?" Marvin cried.

"Alas, my good friend," said the hapless Gules, "it is a knavery so clearcut and so logical as to be irrefutable; and yet so cunning wrought and executed as to make lesser schemes of littler men seem very foolings of most childlike boys. . . . Did you know that I am a member of that secret organization known as the Gray Knights of the Holy Subsidence?"

"Me knew this not," Marvin said. "And yet, the Gray

Knights have ever been friends to learning and companions to piety, and most especially they have espoused 'gainst royal opposition, the cause of d'Augustin."

"True, most extremely true," the miserable Gules said, his weakly handsome features twisted into a grimace of agony. "And so I too believed. But then last day yesterweek I learned that our Grand Master Helvetius had passed away—"

"Due to a bit of steel in the liver," Blackamoor said.

"—and that I was now bound to the new Grand Master, as utterly and completely as ever, since our vows are to the Office, not the man."

"And that new Master?" Marvin asked.

"Happens to be myself!" cried Blackamoor. And now Marvin saw upon his finger the great signet ring of the Order.

"Yes, so it did befall," Blackamoor said, the left side of his mouth twisting cynically. "I appropriated that ancient office, since it was an instrument well suited to my hand and sensible to my usages. And so I am Master, and sole arbiter of Polity and Decision-Making, responsible to no power save that of Hell itself, and answerable to no voice save that which echoes from the nethermost crevices of mine own soul!"

There was something magnificent about Blackamoor at that moment. Detestable and cruel though he was, reactionary and self-involved, luxuriating and careless of others, yet still withal, here was a man. So Marvin thought, with grudging respect. And his mouth hardened into fighting lines as he turned to face his antagonist.

"And now," Blackamoor said, "our principals are upon the stage, and we lack but one actor to fulfill our drama and bring it to a meet conclucence. And this, our last

190

performer, has long and patiently waited in the wings, observing yet unobserved, watching the convolutions of our situation and awaiting his cue to bring him on for his brief moment of glory. . . . But soft, he comes!"

There was a sound of heavy footsteps in the corridor. Those within the room listened and waited, shuffling uneasily. Slowly the door swung open—

And there entered a masked man, clad in black from tip to toe, and carrying over his shoulder a great double-edged axe. He stood poised in the doorway as though unsure of his welcome.

"Good-day to you, executioner," Blackamoor drawled. "Now all is complete, and the final moments of this farce can be performed. Forward, guards!"

The guards closed in the locked sword-mattocks. They seized Marvin and gripped him fast, bending his head forward with neck exposed.

"Executioner!" cried Blackamoor. "Perform your duty!"

The executioner stepped forward and tested the edges of his great axe. He drew the weapon high over his head, stood poised for a moment, then began his downward swing—

And Cathy screamed!

She threw herself upon that grim masked figure, clawing at him, deflecting his heavy axe, which clashed against the granite floor and drew a shower of sparks. The axeman pushed her angrily away, but her fingers had closed around the black silk of his mask.

The executioner roared as he felt the mask being torn away. With a cry of dismay he tried to cover his features. But all in that dungeon room had seen him clear.

Marvin was at first unable to believe the testimony of

his senses. For, beneath that mask, he looked into a face that seemed somehow familiar. Where had he gazed upon that line of cheek and brow, those brown eyes with their faint tilt, that firm jaw?

Then he remembered; he had seen it, long ago, in a mirror.

The executioner was wearing his face, and walking in his body. . . .

"Ze Kraggash!" Marvin said.

"At your service." And the man who had stolen Marvin's body bowed mockingly, and grinned at Marvin with his own face.

CHAPTER 30

LORD BLACKAMOOR WAS FIRST TO BREAK tableau. With skilled fingers he swept off his cap and wig. Loosening his collar, he probed along his neck, unfastening several invisible holders. Then, with a single movement, he peeled the tight-fitting skin mask from his face.

"Detective Urdorf!" Marvin cried.

"Yes, it is I," the Martian detective said. "I am sorry we had to put you through this, Marvin; but it was our best opportunity of bringing your case to a quick and successful conclusion. My colleagues and I decided—"

"Colleagues?" Marvin asked.

"I forgot to make the introductions," Detective Urdorf said, grinning wryly. "Marvin, I would like you to meet Lieutenant Ourie and Sergeant Fraff."

The two who had masqueraded as Lord Inglenook and Sir Gules now swept off their skin-masks and revealed themselves in the uniforms of the Northwest Galactic

193

Interstellar Constabulary. They grinned good-naturedly as they shook Marvin's hand.

"And these gentlemen," Urdorf said, gesturing at the Thuringian guards, "have also aided us considerably."

The guards removed their deal-colored half-jackets of buff, and stood revealed in the orange uniforms of Cassem City Traffic Patrolmen.

Marvin turned to Cathy. She had already pinned to her bodice the red and blue badge of a special agent in the Interplanetary Vigilance Association.

"I—I think I understand," Marvin said.

"It's really simple enough," Detective Urdorf said. "In working on your case, I had, as is usual, the aid and cooperation of various other law enforcement agencies. Upon three separate occasions we came close to capturing our man; but always he evaded us. This might have gone on indefinitely had we not tried this scheme of entrapment. The theory was sound; for if Kraggash could succeed in destroying you, he could claim your body as his own without fear of a counterclaimant. Whereas, as long as you were alive, you would continue to search for him.

"Thus, we enticed you into our scheme, hoping that Kraggash would take notice, and would enter the plan himself so as to be sure of destroying you. The rest is history."

Turning to the unfrocked executioner, Detective Urdorf said, "Kraggash, have you anything to add?"

The thief with Marvin's face lounged gracefully against the wall, his arms folded and his body replete with composure.

"I might hazard a comment or two," Kraggash said. "First, let me point out that your scheme was clumsy and transparent. I believed it to be a hoax from the start, and entered it only on the distant possibility of its being true. Therefore, I am not surprised at this outcome."

"An amusing rationalization," Urdorf said.

Kraggash shrugged. "Secondly, I want to tell you that I feel no moral compunction in the slightest at my so-called crime. If a man cannot retain control of his own body, then he deserves to lose it. I have observed, during a long and varied lifetime, that men will give their bodies to any rogue who asks, and will enslave their minds to the first voice that commands them to obey. This is why the vast majority of men cannot keep even their natural birthright of a mind and body, but choose instead to rid themselves of those embarrassing emblems of freedom."

"That," Detective Urdorf said, "is the classic *apologia* of the criminal."

"That which you call a crime when one man does it," Kraggash said, "you call government when many men do it. Personally, I fail to see the distinction; and failing to see it, I refuse to live by it."

"We could stand here all year splitting words," Detective Urdorf said. "But I do not have time for such recreation. Try your arguments on the prison chaplain, Kraggash. I hereby arrest you for illegal Mindswapping, attempted murder, and grand larceny. Thus I solve my 159th case and break my chain of bad luck."

"Indeed?" Kraggash said coolly. "Did you really think it would be so simple? Or did you consider the possibility that the fox might have another lair?"

"Take him!" Urdorf shouted. The four policemen moved swiftly toward Kraggash. But even as they moved, the criminal raised his hand and drew a swift circle in the air.

195

The circle glowed with fire!

Kraggash put one leg over the circle. His leg disappeared. "If you want me," he said mockingly, "you'll know where to find me."

As the policemen rushed him, he stepped into the circle, and all of him vanished except his head. He winked at Marvin. Then his head was gone, and nothing was left except the circle of fire.

"Come on!" Marvin shouted. "Let's get him!"

He turned to Urdorf, and was amazed to see that the detective's shoulders had slumped, and that his face was gray with defeat.

"Hurry!" Marvin cried.

"It is useless," Urdorf said. "I thought I was prepared for any ruse . . . but not for this. The man is obviously insane."

"What can we do?" Marvin shouted.

"We can do nothing," Urdorf said. "He has gone into the Twisted World, and I have failed in my 159th case."

"But we can still follow him!" Marvin declared, moving up to the fiery circle.

"No! You must not!" Urdorf declared. "You do not understand—the Twisted World means death, or madness . . . or both! Your chances of coming through it are so small—"

"I have just as good a chance as Kraggash!" Marvin shouted, and stepped into the circle.

"Wait, you still do not understand!" Urdorf shouted. "Kraggash *has no chance!*"

But Marvin did not hear those final words, for he had already vanished through the flaming circle, moving inexorably into the strange and unexplored reaches of the Twisted World.

196

CHAPTER 31

SOME EXPLANATIONS OF THE TWISTED WORLD

. . . thus, through the Riemann-Hake equations, a mathematical demonstration existed at last of the theoretical necessity for Twistermann's Spatial Area of Logical Deformation. This Area became known as the Twisted World, though it was neither twisted nor a world. And, by a final irony, Twistermann's all-important third definition (that the Area could be considered as that region of the universe which acted as an equipoise of chaos to the logical stability of the primary reality structure) was proven superfluous.

ARTICLE ON "THE TWISTED WORLD," FROM THE *Galactic Encyclopedia of Universal Knowledge*, 483RD EDITION.

. . . therefore the term *mirror-deformation* carries the sense (if not the substance), of our thought. For indeed, as we have seen, the Twisted World [sic] performs the work, both necessary and hateful, of rendering indeterminate all entities and processes, and thereby making the universe theoretically as well as practically ineluctable.

FROM *Musings of a Mathematician,* EDGAR HOPE GRIEF, EUCLID CITY FREE PRESS.

. . . but despite this, a few tentative rules might be adduced for the suicidal traveler to the Twisted World:

Remember that all rules may lie, in the Twisted World, including this rule which points out the exception, and including this modifying clause which invalidates the exception . . . ad infinitum.

But also remember that no rule *necessarily* lies; that any rule may be true, including this rule and its exceptions.

In the Twisted World, time need not follow your preconceptions. Events may change rapidly (which seems proper), or slowly (which feels better), or not at all (which is hateful).

It is conceivable that *nothing whatsoever* will happen to you in the Twisted World. It would be unwise to expect this, and equally unwise to be unprepared for it.

Among the kingdoms of probability that the Twisted World sets forth, one must be exactly like our World; and another must be exactly like our world except for one detail; and another exactly like ours except for two details; and so forth. And also—

one must be completely *unlike* our world except for one detail; and so forth.

The problem is always prediction: how to tell what world you are in before the Twisted World reveals it disastrously to you.

In the Twisted World, as in any other, you are apt to discover yourself. But only in the Twisted World is that meeting usually fatal.

Familiarity breeds shock—in the Twisted World.

The Twisted World may conveniently, (but incorrectly) be thought of as a reversed world of Maya, of illusion. You may find that the shapes around you are real, while You, the examining consciousness, are illusion. Such a discovery is enlightening, albeit mortifying.

A wise man once asked, "What would happen if I could enter the Twisted World without preconceptions?" A final answer to his question is impossible; but we would hazard that he would have some preconceptions by the time he came out. Lack of opinion is not armor.

Some men feel that the height of intelligence is the discovery that all things may be reversed, and thereby become their opposites. Many clever games can be played with this proposition, but we do not advocate its use in the Twisted World. There all doctrines are equally arbitrary, including the doctrine of the arbitrariness of doctrines.

Do not expect to outwit the Twisted World. It is bigger, smaller, longer and shorter than you; it does not prove; it is.

Something that *is* never has to prove anything.

All proofs are attempts at becoming. A proof is true only to itself, and it implies nothing except the existence of proofs, which prove nothing.

Anything that *is*, is improbable, since everything is extraneous, unnecessary, and a threat to the reason.

Three comments concerning the Twisted World may have nothing to do with the Twisted World. The traveler is warned.

FROM *The Inexorability of the Specious*, BY ZE KRAG-GASH; FROM THE MARVIN FLYNN MEMORIAL COLLECTION.

CHAPTER 32

THE TRANSITION WAS ABRUPT, AND NOT AT all what Marvin thought it would be. He had heard stories about the Twisted World, and had hazily expected to find a place of melting shapes and shifting colors, of grotesques and marvels. But he saw at once that his viewpoint had been romantic and limited.

He was in a small waiting room. The air was stuffy with sweat and steam heat, and he sat on a long wooden bench with several dozen other people. Bored-looking clerks strolled up and down, consulting papers, and occasionally calling for one of the waiting people. Then there would be a whispered conference. Sometimes a man would lose patience and leave. Sometimes a new applicant would arrive.

Marvin waited, watched, daydreamed. Time passed slowly, the room grew shadowy, someone switched on overhead lights. Still no one called his name. Marvin glanced at the men on either side of him, bored rather than curious.

The man on his left was very tall and cadaverous, with an inflamed boil on his neck where the collar rubbed. The man on his right was short and fat and red-faced, and he wheezed with every breath.

"How much longer do you think it should take?" Marvin asked the fat man, more to pass the time than in a serious attempt to gain knowledge.

"Long? How long?" the fat man said. "*Damned* long, that's how long it'll take. You can't hurry their goddamned majesties here in the Automobile Bureau, not even when all you want is to have a perfectly ordinary driver's license renewed, which is what I'm here for."

The cadaverous man laughed: a sound like a stick of wood rapping against an empty gasoline can.

"You'll wait a goddamned long time, baby," he said, "since you happen to be sitting in the Department of Welfare, Small Accounts Division."

Marvin spat thoughtfully on the dusty floor and said, "It happens that both of you gentlemen are wrong. We are seated in the Department, in the *anteroom* of the Department, to be precise, of the Department of Fisheries, I was trying to say. And in my opinion it is a pretty state of affairs when a citizen and taxpayer cannot even go fishing in a tax-supported body of water without wasting half a day or more applying for a license."

The three glared at each other. (There are no heroes in the Twisted World, damned few promises, a mere scattering of viewpoints, and not a conclusion in a carload.)

They stared at each other with not particularly wild surmise. The cadaverous man began to bleed slightly

202

from the fingertips. Marvin and the fat man frowned with embarrassment and affected not to notice. The cadaverous man jauntily thrust his offending hand into a waterproof pocket. A clerk came over to them.

"Which of you is James Grinnell Starmacher?" the clerk asked.

"That's me," Marvin replied. "And I want to say that I've been waiting here for some little time, and I think this department is run in quite an inefficient fashion."

"Yeah, well," the clerk said, "it's because we haven't got in the machines yet." He glanced at his papers. "You have made application for a corpse?"

"That is correct," Marvin said.

"And you affirm that said corpse will not be used for immoral purposes?"

"I so affirm."

"Kindly state your reasons for acquiring this corpse."

"I wish to use it in a purely decorative capacity."

"Your qualifications?"

"I have studied interior decorating."

"State the name and/or identification code number of the most recent corpse obtained by you."

"Cockroach," Marvin replied, "Brood number 3/32/ A45345."

"Killed by?"

"Myself. I am licensed to kill all creatures not of my subspecies, with certain exceptions, such as the golden eagle and the manatee."

"The purpose of your last killing?"

"Ritual purification."

"Request granted," the clerk said. "Choose your corpse."

The fat man and the cadaverous man looked at him

with wet, hopeful eyes. Marvin was tempted, but managed to resist. He turned and said to the clerk, "I choose you."

"It shall be so noted," the clerk said, scribbling on his papers. His face changed to the face of the pseudo-Flynn. Marvin borrowed a crosscut saw from the cadaverous man, and, with some difficulty, cut the clerk's right arm from his body. The clerk expired unctuously, his face changing once again to his clerk's face.

The fat man laughed at Marvin's discomfiture. "A little transsubstantiality goes a long way," he sneered. "But not far enough, eh? Desire shapes flesh, but death is the final sculptor."

Marvin was crying. The cadaverous man touched his arm in a kindly manner. "Don't take it so hard, kid. Symbolic revenge is better than no revenge at all. Your plan was good; its flaw was external to yourself. I am James Grinnell Starmacher."

"I am a corpse," said the corpse of the clerk. "Transposed revenge is better than no revenge at all."

"I came here to renew my driving license," the fat man said. "To hell with all you deep thinkers, how about a little service?"

"Certainly, sir," said the corpse of the clerk. "But in my present condition, I can license you only to fish for dead fish."

"Dead, alive, what difference does it make?" the fat man said. "Fishing is the thing; it doesn't matter so much what you catch."

He turned to Marvin, perhaps to amplify that statement. But Marvin had left and, after an unpersuasive transition, found himself in a large, square, empty room. The walls were made of steel plates, and the ceiling was a hundred feet above his head. There were floodlights up there, and a glassed-in control booth. Peering at him through the glass was Kraggash.

"Experiment 342," Kraggash intoned crisply. "Subject: Death. Proposition: Can a human being be killed? Remarks: This question concerning the possible mortality of human beings has long perplexed our finest thinkers. A considerable folklore has sprung up around the subject of death, and unverified reports of *killings* have been made throughout the ages. Furthermore, corpses have been brought forth from time to time, indubitably dead, and represented as the remains of human beings. Despite the ubiquity of these corpses, no causal link has ever been proven to show that they ever lived, much less that they were once human beings. Therefore, in an attempt to settle the question once and for all, we have set up the following experiment. Step one . . ."

A steel plate in the wall flew back on its hinge. Marvin whirled in time to see a spear thrust forth at him. He sidestepped, made clumsy by his lame foot, and evaded the thrust.

More plates popped open. Knives, arrows, clubs, all were flung at him from various angles.

A poison-gas generator was pushed through an opening. A tangle of cobras was dropped into the room. A lion and a tank bounded forward. A blowgun hissed. Energy weapons crackled. Flamethrowers coughed. A mortar cleared its throat.

Water flooded the room, rising quickly. Naphtha fire poured down from the ceiling.

But the fire burned the lions, which ate the snakes, which clogged the howitzers, which crushed the spears, which jammed the gas generator, which dissolved the water, which quenched the fire.

Marvin stood forth miraculously unscathed. He shook his fist at Kraggash, slipped on the steel plating, fell and broke his neck.

He was afforded a military funeral with full honors. His widow died with him on the flaming pyre. Kraggash tried to follow, but was refused the solace of suttee.

Marvin lay in the tomb for three days and three nights, during which time his nose dripped continuously. His entire life passed before his eyes in slow motion. At the end of that time he arose and moved onward.

There were five objects of limited but undeniable sentience in a place with no qualities worth mentioning. One of these objects was, presumably, Marvin. The other four were lay figures, hastily sketched stereotypes designed for the sole purpose of adorning the primary situation. The problem confronting the five was, which of them was Marvin, and which were the unimportant background figures?

First came a question of nomenclature. Three of the five wished to be called Marvin immediately, one wanted to be called Edgar Floyd Morrison, and one wished to be referred to as "unimportant background figure."

This was quite obviously tendentious, and so they numbered themselves from one to four, the fifth stubbornly insisting upon being called Kelly.

"All right, already," said Number One, who had already taken on officious air. "Gentlemen, could we maybe stop beating our gums and bring this meeting to order?"

"A Jewish accent won't help you here," Number Three said darkly.

"Look," said Number One, "what would a Polack know about Jewish accents? As it happens, I am Jewish only on my father's side, and although I esteem—"

"Where am I?" said Number Two. "My God, what happened to me? Ever since I left Stanhope . . ."

"Shut up, Wop," Number Four said.

"My name-a not Wop, my name-a she'sa Luigi," Number Two responded swarthily. "I bin two year in your greata country ever' since I leetle boy in village San Minestrone della Zuppa, nicht wahr?"

"Sheet, man," Number Three said darkly. "You ain't no dagowop atall nohow, you ain't nuttin but jes' a plain ornary privisional background figure of limited flexibility; so suppose you jes shut you mouf afore I do dat little ting for you, nicht wahr?"

"Listen," said Number One, "I'm a simple man of simple tastes and if it'll help any I'll give up my rights to Marvinhood."

"Memory, memory," muttered Number Two. "What has happened to me? Who are these apparitions, these talkative shades?"

"Oh, I say!" Kelly said. "That's really bad form, old man!"

"It'sa pretty goddamn disingenuous," muttered Luigi.

"Invocation is *not* convocation," said Number Three.

"But I really don't remember," said Number Two.

"So I don't remember so good neither," said Number

One. "But do you hear me making a big thing out of it? I'm not even claiming to be human. The mere fact that I can recite Leviticus by heart don't prove nothing."

"Too right it doesn't!" shouted Luigi. "And disproof don't prove any flaming thing neither."

"I thought you were supposed to be Italian," Kelly said to him.

"I am, but I was raised in Australia. It's rather a strange story—"

"No stranger than mine," Kelly said. "Black Irishman do you call me? But few know that I passed my formative years in a Hangchow whorehouse, and that I enlisted in the Canadian army to escape French persecution for my part in aiding the Gaullists in Mauretania; and that is why—"

"Zut, alors!" cried Number Four. "One can keep silence no longer! To question my credentials is one thing; to asperse my country is another!"

"Yer indignation don't prove a thing!" Number Three cried. "Not that I really care, since I choose no longer to be Marvin."

"Passive resistance is a form of aggression," Number Four responded.

"Inadmissable evidence is still a form of evidence," Three retorted.

"I don't know what any of you are talking about," Number Two declared.

"Ignorance will get you nowhere," Number Four snarled. "I refuse categorically to be Marvin."

"You can't give up what you haven't got," Kelly said archly.

"I can give up anything I damned well want to!"

Number Four cried passionately. "I not only give up my Marvinity; I also step down from the throne of Spain, yield up the dictatorship of the Inner Galaxy, and renounce my salvation in Bahai."

"Feel better now, kid?" Luigi asked sardonically.

"Yes . . . It was insupportable. Simplification suits my intricate nature," Number Four said. "Which of you is Kelly?"

"I am," Kelly said.

"Do you realize," Luigi asked him, "that only you and I have names?"

"That's true," Kelly said. "You and I are different!"

"Here now, just a moment!" Number One said.

"Time, gentlemen, time, please!"

"Hold the fort!"

"Hold your water!"

"Hold the phone!"

"As I was saying," Luigi said. "We! Us! The Named Ones of the Proof Presumptive! Kelly—you can be Marvin if I can be Kraggash!"

"Done!" roared Kelly, over the protests of the lay figures.

Marvin and Kraggash grinned at each other in the momentary euphoria of identity-intoxication. Then they flung themselves at each other's throats. Manual strangulation followed apace. The three numbered ones, robbed of a birthright they had never possessed, took up conventional poses of stylized ambiguity. The two lettered ones, granted an identity they had seized anyhow, tore and bit at each other, flung forth defiant arias and cringed before devastating recitatives. Number One watched until he grew bored, then began playing with a lap dissolve.

That did it. The whole shooting works slid away like a greased pig on roller skates coming down a solid glass mountain, only slightly faster.

Day succeeded night, which succeeded in making a perfect fool of itself.

Plato wrote: "It ain't whatcha do, it's the way thatcha do it." Then, deciding that the world was not yet ready for this, he scrubbed it out.

Hammurabi wrote: "The unexamined life is not worth living." But he wasn't sure it was true, so he scratched it out.

Gautama Buddha wrote: "Brahmins stink." But later he revised it.

Nature abhors a vacuum, and I don't like it much either. Marvinissimo! Here he comes catfooting along, flaunting his swollen identity. All men are mortal, he tells us, but some are more mortal than others. There he is, playing in the backyard, making value judgments out of mud. Having no respect, he becomes his father. Last week we revoked his Godhead; we caught him operating a life without a license.

(But I have warned you often, my friends, of the Protoplasmic Peril. It creeps across the heavens, extinguishing stars. Shamelessly it survives and flows, uprooting planets and smothering the stars. With damnable insistence it deposits its abominations.)

He comes again, that seedy juggler in an off-beige skin,

that monstrous optimist with the stitched smile! Killer, kill thyself! Burglar, steal thyself! Fisher, catch thyself! Farmer, harvest thyself!

And now we will hear the report of the Special Investigator.

"Thank you, ahem. I have found that Marvin is the one to have when you're having more than one; that stars fell on Marvin Flynn; that one should praise the Lord and pass the Marvin Flynn. And I have also noted: Darling, as long as you're up, get me a Marvin Flynn. Marvin Flynn is actually better than the higher-priced spread. Promise her anything, but give her Marvin Flynn. You have a friend at Marvin Flynn. Let your Marvin do the walking through the Yellow Pages. Drink Marvin—it satisfies! Why not worship this week at the Marvin Flynn of your choice? For the Marvin Flynn that prays together stays together."

. . . were locked in titanic combat, which, since it had happened, was inevitable. Marvin smote Kraggash upon the breastbone, then smote him again most grievously upon the nose bone. Kraggash promptly changed into Ireland, which Marvin invaded as a demi-legion of Danish berserkers, forcing Kraggash to attempt a kingside pawnstorm, which stood no chance against a low flush. Marvin reached for his opponent, missed, and devastated Atlantis. Kraggash swung backhanded and slaughtered a gnat.

Deadly the battle raged across the steaming swamps of the Miocene; a colony of termites mourned their queen as Kraggash cometed helplessly into Marvin's sun, fragmenting at last into countless militant spores. But Marvin

211

unerringly picked the diamond from the glittering glass, and Kraggash fell back upon Gibraltar.

His bastion fell in a night when Marvin kidnapped the Barbary apes, and Kraggash speeded across southern Thrace with his body in a suitcase. He was seized at the frontier of Phthistia, a country that Marvin improvised with considerable effect upon the history of Europe.

Weakening, Kraggash became evil; becoming evil, Kraggash grew weak. In vain he invented devil-worship. The followers of Marvinity bowed down not to the idol, but rather to the symbol. Evil, Kraggash turned nasty: dirt grew beneath his fingernails, noxious tufts of hair appeared on his soul.

Helpless at last Kraggash lay, the incarnation of evil, with the body of Marvin clutched in his talon. Rites of exorcism induced his final agony. A buzz saw disguised as a prayer wheel dismembered him, a mace masquerading as a censer brained him. Kindly old Father Flynn intoned over him the last words: "Thou gettest no bread with one meatball." And Kraggash was put into a tomb hewn out of the living Kraggash. Appropriate graffiti were carved upon his tombstone, and flowering Kraggash was planted around his grave.

It is a quiet spot. To the left is a grove of Kraggash trees, to the right is an oil refinery. Here is an empty beer can, here is a gypsy moth. And just beyond is the spot where Marvin opened the suitcase and took out his long-lost body.

He blew the dust off it and combed its hair. He wiped its nose and straightened its tie. Then, with seemly reverence, he put it on.

CHAPTER 33

AND THUS MARVIN FLYNN FOUND HIMSELF
back on Earth and inside his own body. He went to
his hometown of Stanhope, and found things unchanged.
The town was still some three hundred miles from New
York in physical distance, and some hundred years away
in spiritual and emotional distance. Just as before there
were the orchards, and the clusters of brown cows grazing against the rolling green pastureland. Eternal was the
elm-lined main street and the lonely late-night wail of a
jetliner.

No one asked Marvin where he had been. Not even his
best friend, Billy Hake, who assumed he had taken a
jaunt to one of the regular tourist spots, like Sinkiang or
the lower Ituri Rain Forest.

At first, Marvin found this invincible stability as upset-
ting as he had ever found the transpositions of Mindswap
or the deformed conundrums of the Twisted World. Sta-

213

bility seemed exotic to him; he kept on waiting for it to fade away.

But places like Stanhope do not fade, and boys like Marvin gradually lose their sense of enchantment and high purpose.

Alone late at night in his attic room, Marvin often dreamed of Cathy. He still found it difficult to think of her as a special agent of the Interplanetary Vigilance Association. And yet, there had been a hint of officiousness in her manner, and a glint of the righteous prosecutor in her beautiful eyes.

He loved her and would always mourn her loss; but he was more content to mourn her than to possess her. And, if the truth must be told, Marvin's eye had already been caught, or recaptured, by Marsha Baker, the demure and attractive young daughter of Edwin Marsh Baker, Stanhope's leading real-estate dealer.

Stanhope, if not the best of all possible worlds, was still the best world Marvin had seen. It was a place where you could live without things' jumping out at you, and without your jumping out at things. No metaphoric deformation was possible in Stanhope; a cow looked exactly like a cow, and to call it anything else was unwarrantable poetic license.

And so, undoubtedly: east, west, home's the best; and Marvin set himself the task of enjoyment of the familiar, which sentimental wise men say is the apex of human wisdom.

His life was marred only by one or two small doubts. First and foremost was the question: How had he come back to Earth from the Twisted World?

He did considerable research on this question, which

214

was more ominous than it first seemed. He realized that nothing is impossible in the Twisted World, and that nothing is even improbable. There is causality in the Twisted World, but there is also noncausality. Nothing *must* be; nothing is *necessary*. Because of this, it was quite conceivable that the Twisted World had flung him back to Earth, showing its power by relinquishing its power over Marvin.

That indeed seemed to be what had happened. But there was another, less pleasant alternative.

This was expressed in the Doormhan Propositions as follows: "Among the kingdoms of probability that the Twisted World sets forth, one must be exactly like our world, and another must be exactly like our world except for one detail, and another exactly like our world except for two details, and so forth."

Which meant that he might still be on the Twisted World, and that this Earth which he perceived might be no more than a passing emanation, a fleeting moment of order in the fundamental chaos, destined to be dissolved at any moment back into the fundamental senselessness of the Twisted World.

In a way it made no difference, since nothing is permanent except our illusions. But no one likes to have his illusions threatened, and Marvin wanted to know where he stood.

Was he on Earth, or was he on a replica of Earth?

Might there not be some significant detail inconsistent with the Earth he had left? Might there not be several details? Marvin tried to find out for the sake of his peace of mind. He explored Stanhope and its environs, looked and tested and checked the flora and fauna.

Nothing seemed to be amiss. Life went on as usual; his father tended his herds of rats, and his mother placidly continued to lay eggs.

He went north to Boston and New York, then farther south to the vast Philadelphia–Los Angeles area. Everything seemed in order. He contemplated crossing the continent on the mighty Delaware River and continuing his search in the California cities of Schenectady, Milwaukee, and Shanghai.

He changed his mind, however, realizing that there was no sense in spending his life trying to discover whether or not he had a life to spend.

Besides, there was the possibility that, even if the Earth were changed, his memory and perceptions might also be changed, rendering discovery impossible.

He lay beneath Stanhope's familiar green sky and considered this possibility. It seemed unlikely: for did not the giant oak trees still migrate each year to the south? Did not the huge red sun move across the sky, pursued by its dark companion? Did not the triple moons return each month with their new accumulation of comets?

These familiar sights reassured him. Everything seemed to be as it always had been. And so, willingly and with a good grace, Marvin accepted his world at face value, married Marsha Baker, and lived forever after.